SILVER BELLS AT
MOONGLOW

SILVER BELLS AT MOONGLOW

A Moonglow Christmas Novella

DEBORAH GARNER

CRANBERRY COVE PRESS

Cranberry Cove Press
PO Box 1671
Jackson, WY 83001, United States

Library of Congress Catalog-in-Publication Data Available
Garner, Deborah
Silver Bells at Moonglow / Deborah Garner—1st United States edition
1. Fiction 2. Woman Authors 3. Holidays

p. cm.
ISBN-13:
978-0-9969960-1-3 (paperback)
978-0-9969960-9-9 (hardback)

Printed in the United States of America
10 9 8 7 6 5 4 3 2

For my mother,
who always made holidays special for us.

ONE

Mist stood in the doorway of the Timberton Hotel, looking out at the empty street. It had been a lively scene earlier that day, filled with cheerful faces as the small-town residents exchanged secret gifts with each other. This had been Marge's idea. Betty, the hotelkeeper, had at first thought it simply a clever way for Marge to unburden herself of an item collecting dust on a shelf. Betty knew Marge had a habit of frequenting the town thrift shop, always emerging with a purchase or two whether she needed anything or not. Others in the town suspected the same motive behind the first annual "Secret Santa" exchange. Each person who participated in the holiday activity had thrown a name into a hat and pulled another out, all hoping to avoid the inevitable thrift shop item. Mist smiled, remembering a fleeting look of dismay on Clayton's face when Marge handed the fire captain a small box at the exchange. His polite, courteous expression had turned into a huge grin when he discovered a batch of mint-chocolate fudge from her candy store.

Others had been pleased with their gifts as well. Millie, the town librarian, had received a hand-embroidered bookmark from Betty. Clive, who ran the local sapphire gallery, was thrilled with the fine bottle of whiskey from Ernie, the night bartender at Pop's Parlor. Mist, who had chosen not to draw a name, presented Hollister, the quietest town resident, with a set of watercolor paints. William Guthrie, owner of the greasy spoon, "Wild Bill's," had then surprised Mist with a petite bouquet of flowers from Maisie's Daisies, telling her it was a thank-you for letting him escape his own cooking.

All in all, it was a good start to a holiday weekend that promised to be eventful. With Christmas just three days away, the small Montana town of Timberton was gearing up for several annual holiday celebrations. Betty's cookie exchange, a highlight of the season, was held each year at the hotel. Town residents always managed to come up with a few delicious new concoctions, in addition to regular favorites. This traditional gathering promised to be upstaged only by the feast to be served in the hotel's café, Moonglow, on Christmas Eve. Mist, well-known as Timberton's local chef and artist, resided at the hotel, where the café was conveniently located.

Mist stepped back inside the hotel and gently closed the door, setting off a brief jingling of bells from a wreath. She took a deep breath and closed her eyes, taking in the silence that followed. The only guests who'd already arrived for the holiday were resting in their room after a tiring flight from Philadelphia. Winter travel could be especially challenging, and Christopher and Michelle Callahan had faced the worst of it—cancelled flights, rerouting, a night spent in the Denver airport, and lost luggage, on top of it all. Mist had steeped a pot of chamomile tea and placed a cup of it on Mrs. Callahan's nightstand, along with a forehead-width sachet pillow filled with lavender. The woman had thanked her profusely and excused herself for a well-deserved evening of rest. Betty had stepped out on an errand, vowing to rest up for the busy weekend as soon as she returned. Mist was pleased to hear the hotelkeeper planned to take a break from preholiday preparations. As much as Mist tried to handle most of the hotel's upkeep, Betty insisted on doing her share.

The soft, under-counter lights in the hotel kitchen felt soothing as Mist stepped into the room. Although she utilized the bright, overhead light for meal preparation, the absence of it offered a peaceful ambiance for evening planning. Even the action of turning the main light off after the dinner hour signaled a shift to a different portion of the day. This was her own time, her time to contemplate and look forward. She poured herself a cup from the pot of chamomile tea and pulled out the registration book, looking over the upcoming arrivals.

There would be ten guests joining them for Christmas this year, some returning, some new. Hotel guests, that is. Timberton townsfolk would flock to the hotel daily, whether for a festive Christmas Eve dinner in the Moonglow café, or to participate in Betty's annual cookie exchange, or merely to comingle in the spirit of the holidays. And there was always the temptation of enjoying a glazed cinnamon nut, or three, from the bowl Betty kept in the front parlor. That alone brought local residents in and out of the hotel. However, ten would be overnight guests, counting the Callahans. Belinda Myers would be a first-timer, and Mist knew little about her, only that someone else had made the reservation for her and that she was coming in from California. Three other guests were first-timers, as well, all sisters, each traveling from different areas, meeting up for a holiday reunion. Betty had warned Mist the sisters had been calling independently of each other with requests, and that it might take some maneuvering to meet all their needs.

And then there was Michael Blanton.

Mist closed the registration book and pictured the young man the previous year, sitting by the fireplace, reading. Of all the prior guests, his image was the clearest in her mind: lanky, relatively tall, with medium brown hair and the most unusual eyes she had ever seen. *Patina*, she thought, looking back. That was the description she'd come up with for the gray-green-coppery color of his eyes. He'd questioned whether or not that could even be a color—patina— and she had explained that, of course, a color could be anything. After all, it could be, as far as she was concerned—texture, sound, perhaps even the wind.

It surprised her—or did it—to acknowledge she'd been looking forward to Michael Blanton's return. They had connected the year before in an unexplainable way, kindred spirits of an undefined sort. Was it their mutual interest in literature? Or the way he seemed to understand what she meant when others were baffled by her new-age view of the world? So many things about life seemed clear to her, but this did not.

At the sound of footsteps outside the kitchen's side door, Mist closed the registration book and took a sip of tea. As expected, Betty stepped through the door, speckles of snow covering her knit winter hat and a recognizable bag from the candy shop clutched inside a red mitten.

"Let me guess… caramels?" Mist said, already knowing the answer. She smiled. It was common knowledge that Betty often took a short walk to Marge's candy store to pick up her favorite addiction.

"I can't believe you even guessed," Betty teased. She set the bag of caramels on the kitchen counter and removed her coat, hat, and gloves, hanging them on a hook behind the door before switching on a coffeemaker, already preset. Turning toward Mist, she ran her hands over her plump hips, smoothing out a lengthy red sweater that had crumpled under her coat. Mist adored Betty's casual attire, always slightly old-fashioned yet not frumpy. It suited her senior status and friendly yet calm personality.

Mist took a final sip of tea, then stood and placed her cup in the sink. Returning to the center island counter, she sat back down, her jewel-toned gauze skirt flowing over the side of the stool. She pulled her purple ballet flats up onto a lower rung, adjusted her balance, and pulled a binder from the side of the table, opening it and looking over her notes.

"Meal planning, I see." Betty observed. "The town can hardly wait to see what you serve for dinner this year, you know. Not that they don't adore everything you serve in your café, but your Christmas Eve dinner is legendary."

"*Our* café," Mist said, directing a soft smile at Betty. "The café is a community area, a place where people can come together and enjoy camaraderie over a meal."

"Yes, dear," Betty said. "I agree. And the town definitely feels that way."

"As they should," Mist said, pleased that those who'd first dined at the Moonglow café simply as a place to get a meal had grown fond of it as a gathering place. This had been Mist's intention all along. Food was a way to bring people together. She'd learned that long ago, back as an art student in Santa Cruz, California, working part-time in a café, where she'd first learned to create culinary delights. Little did she know she'd later move to the small Montana town of Timberton. Or that her food might even work a bit of magic in people's lives.

"So what's on the menu?" Betty poured herself a mug of coffee and took a seat across from Mist. "You've been debating a variety of dishes."

Mist looked over her notes. "I've had trouble deciding, not knowing what this year's guest preferences will be, but I believe I've come to a good balance: some dishes with meat, some vegetarian, plenty of side dishes and, of course, dessert."

"Ah, dessert," Betty said. "You outdid yourself last year with that *Bûche de Noël*. I believe Clive's been yearning for that since last Christmas."

"Perhaps next year," Mist said. "But he'll be pleased with this year's meal, I'm sure."

"Hardly a doubt about that." Betty laughed. "He loves anything you make, just like everyone else in this town. The hotel guests, as well."

"I'm grateful for their compliments," Mist replied. "But much of it is the feeling they get from dining together, the connection."

"I do believe you're right." Betty took a sip of coffee. "I've watched the town come together since you've been here, and much of it seems to happen during meals. Why, look at Maisie and Clayton, for example. They might never have met if not for the café."

Mist smiled and nodded. The romance between Maisie, who ran the flower shop, and Clayton, the fire chief, had been a surprise. They'd met over the Christmas Eve meal the year before, Maisie helping serve and Clayton, as always, sliding in first for a place at the table. It had been charming to watch Maisie casually volunteer to help with meals for the first few months after that dinner. And equally charming to watch the way Clayton started arriving for meals a little more spruced up than usual.

Yes, the Moonglow café worked a little magic, especially during the Christmas season. Which was exactly what Mist intended. And this year promised to be no different. The question was: what small miracles would this year's holiday bring?

TWO

Mist pulled out a sheet of rice paper and a calligraphy pen and began to write.

tarragon
ginger root
garlic
almonds
walnuts
quinoa
fresh cranberries
oranges
pears
mint
baby spinach
tomatoes
shallots
celery
sweet potatoes
zucchini
apples
beets
maple syrup—pure

Moving to the kitchen cupboards, she took a quick inventory of other items she'd need for holiday cooking. Most spices were already in stock. A good supply of flour and sugar always stood ready for morning baking. Only fresh produce and a few other items needed to be picked up in order for her to settle in, knowing she'd be prepared for the next few days.

She hadn't planned a complicated menu, at least not complicated from her perspective. Variety was always a good thing to offer, especially with new guests who might have particular tastes. She wasn't worried about the locals, not after feeding them for over a year. She knew Ernie, the night bartender at Pop's Parlor, was allergic to shellfish. And that Millie, the town librarian, needed gluten-free meals. Even Marge, who owned the candy store, was, ironically, diabetic and always needed more protein and fewer carbs. Mist planned her meals for them accordingly, just as she did for William "Wild Bill" Guthrie, who had been told by his doctor to watch his sodium intake after a recent heart attack. He grumbled about it every time a pretzel or potato chip passed by.

Satisfied she'd planned properly, she closed the cupboards and turned back toward the center of the kitchen, where she found Clive Barnes standing, her list in hand.

"Looks too healthy to me."

"If you'd like, I could fix you a chili dog and cheese fries." Mist smiled, knowing this would actually sound good to Clive, as much as he loved her cooking. "That could be your Christmas Eve dinner," she continued. "Think how jealous the other guests would be while stuck with their own heaping portions of apple-walnut stuffed pork roast, sugar snap peas with orange-maple butter, and sweet potato drizzled with maple syrup. They'd also have to make do with zucchini spice bread instead of your hot dog bun."

Clive paused before speaking up. "Well… maybe I'll save the chili dog and cheese fries for another time, like New Year's Day, in front of a football game?"

"Might be slightly more appropriate," Mist replied nonchalantly, "but entirely up to you."

"She's pulled one over on you again, hmm, Clive?" Betty walked in, a stack of kitchen towels in her hand. She set the freshly laundered linens on the counter and stepped beside Clive, who slid an arm around her waist.

"Sure did, confound it," Clive said. "She'll suggest something that gets my mouth watering and then follow that with some concocted combination of food that I know darn well will be a tastier meal even though I haven't the least idea what half of it is."

"Trying new tastes is one of life's adventures," Mist pointed out.

"I'm not about to argue with that, not after all the dishes of yours I've tried," Clive agreed. "You've opened my eyes up to some mighty fine fixins. There was a time I would have thought pork and apples could only mean a chop and a scoop of applesauce. I don't know what this stuffed thingamabob is that you're planning to serve, but I know enough to expect a step up from a pork chop."

"You're learning, Clive," Betty said. "And you're eating healthier food since Mist came to Timberton. It's good for you."

"Thanks, Betty." Clive smiled sweetly at Betty, then turned toward Mist and whispered. "But I can still have the chili dog and cheese fries on New Year's Day, right?"

"Whatever you want." Mist laughed. She glanced up briefly enough to see Betty elbow Clive. His whispered remark hadn't escaped Betty's keen hearing.

"How about a cup of coffee?" Betty moved to the coffeemaker on the kitchen counter and poured two mugs before Clive even answered. She already knew what his response would be.

"Don't mind if I do," Clive said as expected. He took a seat at the center and smiled up at Betty as she handed him a mug of the fresh-roasted brew.

Mist was delighted to see the two senior lovebirds so happy. Things had certainly changed since she first arrived in the small mountain town, when Betty and Clive had an emotional standoff going on, after years of not acknowledging their mutual feelings.

"Betty," Mist said, "tell me about the three sisters who are coming in for this year's holiday period. Anything I should know?"

"I don't know much," Betty said. "Only bits and pieces from their phone calls. I tell you, it's so much easier when one person in a group coordinates a trip. I never know what one has told another when different people call. Two sounded pleasant on the phone. One was quite abrupt. I know they're all coming in from different parts of the country."

"Yes, I saw that." Mist set aside the shopping list and flipped the registration book open. "One is from

Boston, another from Charleston, and the third from Seattle."

"Almost as if they've purposely spread themselves across the country," Betty said.

"That thought occurred to me," Mist said. "Perhaps they're looking at this get-together as a sort of reunion."

"Ha." Clive snorted. "That could go a couple of different ways, if you ask me."

"I suppose it could," Mist said. "But we can help it sway in a positive direction."

"Well, if anyone can do that, it's you," Betty said. "You're the miracle worker around here."

"That's sweet of you to say, Betty, but it's really not true." Mist had offered up this explanation before. "People work their own miracles; they just don't always know it."

"Whatever you say," Clive said. He downed his coffee, stood up, and headed for the door. "Thanks for the coffee, ladies. I have to get over to open the gallery. Don't want to miss any holiday sales."

"How's your jewelry doing, Clive?" Betty fetched the empty coffee mug and moved it to the kitchen sink. "Those sterling silver pine tree pins with a tiny sapphire at the top were selling well, last I heard."

"That they are, especially the ones with the red sapphires. It always surprises folks to find out not all sapphires are blue." Clive beamed. "But Mist's miniature paintings are also selling well. In fact, I could use some more, if you have any." He turned toward Mist and raised an eyebrow.

"I'll bring a few over later," Mist offered. "I have flowers to pick up at Maisie's this afternoon, which

I'll need to put in water right away. I'll drop some paintings by after that."

"Great. Thank you kindly, Ms. Mist." Clive waved good-bye over his shoulder as he left.

"That's right," Betty said, turning back to Mist. "I can hardly wait to see what you come up with for centerpieces this year. Did Maisie order anything special for you? Do you even know what's coming in?"

Mist shook her head, causing long strands of beaded earrings to brush across her shoulders. "Not really. I put in requests, but some flowers are more difficult to obtain this time of year. We'll see what she brings in. Whatever it is, we'll make it work."

"You'll make it work, all right." Betty laughed. "I have no doubt about that."

THREE

O f all the shops in Timberton, Maisie's Daisies was Mist's favorite, not that she'd want to make a point of that in front of other town businesspeople. Each shop had its own appeal, and the business owners all deserved credit for the services they provided to the community. Marge worked hard to keep her candy shop filled with goodies, much to the delight of many. Ernie showed up promptly each night at Pop's Parlor, filling shot glasses for those looking for something a little more intense than what Marge offered. Sally, who owned the thrift shop "Secondhand Sally's," had upgraded the shop substantially since purchasing the business earlier that year. And locals could always count on catching up on the latest gossip from Glenda while getting a shampoo and style at the Curl 'n Cue.

But Maisie's place offered something entirely unique to Mist. It brought to mind the palette of paints she used for art, except with added dimension. The flowers and foliage touched every sense. She loved the sculpted shape of rose petals, the soft tickle of asparagus ferns, and the sweet fragrance of gardenias. Most of all, she loved the unspoken challenge that Maisie's ever-evolving inventory offered. She could pick and choose different ingredients and, gathering them up in her arms, head back to the hotel to create. The result was always something different, as was to be expected, in Mist's opinion. The ingredients were always unique, the combinations new, and the muse's presence varied. She never knew quite what she'd create at any given time, which was part of the delight.

"There you are," Maisie said as Mist stepped through the front door, a tiny bell signaling her arrival. "I knew you'd be by any time now. I hid a few things for you in back."

"You didn't need to," Mist said. "You know I'm happy to work with whatever you happen to have."

"This time I really did need to hide them. A woman came through a short time ago and started grabbing just about everything in sight."

"That's unusual," Mist said. "Was it Millie, decorating the library, or Glenda, looking to spruce up the beauty salon tables?"

Maisie shook her head. "It wasn't anyone I knew. I'd never seen this woman before. Could be someone new to town, I suppose, or someone simply passing through. She was in a hurry, in fact, downright rude, if you ask me."

"I'm sorry to hear that. Rudeness is even more disagreeable to the person being rude, though that person usually doesn't realize it." Mist paused. "I don't know of anyone new in town. But it's always possible."

Maisie shrugged her shoulders and headed for the back room. "Yep, always possible," she echoed over her shoulders. Mumbled words followed until Maisie reappeared, or at least Maisie's body, with a hefty assortment of flowers and greenery where her face, chest, and shoulders normally would be.

"Why, Maisie," Mist exclaimed slyly. "I don't believe I'll need to arrange anything this year. You—if that *is* you behind that walking forest—can just come over to the hotel and stand in the front parlor, festive as you are."

"Very funny." Maisie laughed. She gently placed the massive bundle of floral items on the counter and blew a wayward leaf off the tip of her nose at the same time. Mist reached over and pulled a cluster of berries out of Maisie's hair, then paused and put it back in.

"What?" Maisie lifted one hand to her head, curious what Mist had found.

"Red berries," Mist explained. "Leave them there. They look seasonally festive with your green hair." Maisie's spiked green hair was a unique sight amidst Timberton's old Western flair.

"Clayton's not too crazy about the green," Maisie said. "I've been thinking about changing it. Plus his parents are coming in Christmas Eve. I've never met them."

"You could try violet," Mist suggested. "Violet offers a sense of truth and authenticity."

"I was thinking more along the lines of brown. As in, my natural color."

"I didn't know green wasn't your natural color," Mist said, her heart warming as she took in the spread of reds, whites, and greens in front of her. "Green is peaceful, refreshing, like the flowers you provide. It suits you. Sometimes we have to choose our own natural colors in life. The ones that help us grow."

"Speaking of choosing…" Maisie hinted. She spread her arms out wide, framing the selection.

"What a wonderful assortment you've brought in," Mist exclaimed. "The white lilies and red hydrangea will make a stunning combination. And those pale green cymbidium orchids! Those will soften the deeper pine shades."

"How about some roses? I know you prefer more exotic flowers, but take a look at the ones in the cooler."

Mist turned to the small refrigerated display. "Definitely some of the white roses. Those will add elegance to the hydrangeas and lilies. I'll pass on the red ones, but I'll take as many of those white button chrysanthemums as you can give me, as well as red berries, spruce, and eucalyptus to work inside the arrangements."

"You need any pinecones, branches, or that type of thing?" Maisie pulled the roses and chrysanthemums from the cooler and wrapped them in paper.

"I saved all the nonperishable decorations from last year," Mist said. "I've been using many in fall arrangements but will rework them all into Christmas displays tonight. We only have one guest arriving this evening. The rest come in tomorrow."

"Betty's annual cookie exchange is tomorrow too, isn't it?"

"Yes, it is," Mist said. "Making this one busy weekend."

"Ooh, count me in on that. I already know I'm bringing snickerdoodles. I'll just have to hide them so they don't disappear before the exchange."

Mist laughed. "Yes, I imagine there will be plenty of hidden cookies around town." She gathered four huge paper bundles into her arms and rested them against her right shoulder, craning her neck around them to bid good-bye to Maisie. "See you at the cookie exchange, if not before. Thank you for bringing in such beautiful ingredients this year."

"Ingredients?" Maisie said, a quizzical expression on her face. "Are you getting confused with the talk about baking?"

"Not at all, Maisie," Mist said, smiling. "Everything is an ingredient of something else. These flowers are ingredients for holiday memories, just like flour and sugar."

* * *

It didn't take long to return to the hotel and run water in the kitchen sink, setting the flowers and greenery from Maisie's in to soak until time to arrange them later.

As Mist expected, Clive was at his work desk when she arrived at the gallery, adding final touches to what she assumed was a new piece of jewelry at first. She crossed the room, set down a tub containing miniature paintings, and took a look.

"Enchanting, Clive," Mist said, eyeing the Christmas ornament with approval. "I love this piece.

Any possibility it's for your gallery shop? Customers would love it. I'm sure it would sell as well as your sapphire pendants."

"Nope, not a chance." Clive shook his head and leaned forward, inspecting the piece closely.

"Ah, I understand." Mist smiled, remembering the ornament Clive had made for Betty the year before. She'd suggested he make others like it to sell at the gallery, but he had been firm that the ornaments he made would be for her. He'd started the collection with a sterling-silver-and-sapphire pine tree. The piece had caught the light beautifully as it dangled from a branch of the main room's Christmas tree. This new ornament would make a lovely addition.

"I know you all felt I should make ornaments to sell here in the gallery as well, but there's only so much time," Clive pointed out. "I'm doing well selling the jewelry, plus I keep busy teaching people about the sapphire mining in the area when they stop by."

"You have a wonderful way with visitors, Clive," Mist said. "I've watched people sort through the gravel, hoping to find sapphires."

"They do love that," Clive agreed. "Every now and then someone comes up with a decent stone. I've designed jewelry around a few of those finds." He sat back and looked around. "Then I've got the art to sell too. Speaking of which…"

"Yes," Mist echoed. "Speaking of which, I have quite a few more paintings for you." She lifted the tub onto a nearby chair, opened the lid, and pulled out a miniature canvas detailing a bird on a snowy tree branch."

"That's a good one," Clive said, nodding his head. "People like that bird. The last one sold right away."

"It's not the same bird," Mist whispered as if telling Clive a secret.

"Huh. Looks the same."

"No bird is the same as another bird," Mist said. "Just as no person is the same as another person."

"Here we go…" Clive sighed.

Mist smiled, knowing Clive was prepared for a dose of Mist's own unique philosophy of life. However, she intended only to give him the paintings he needed to restock the gallery. With flower arrangements, food preparation, and incoming guests, there was plenty of reason to get back to the hotel quickly.

"Here, take a look at the others." Mist pulled out a variety of paintings, most keeping within a seasonal theme. Clusters of pinecones and holly branches, winter scenes of Timberton's Main Street, and snow-flecked Christmas wreathes had all proven to be customer favorites. She'd prepared several of each.

"Perfect," Clive said. "I have a customer who asked for that Main Street scene just the other day. I've been meaning to tell you. I seem to always forget whatever I'm going to say when I'm over at the hotel." He grinned, knowing Mist would catch his meaning.

"That's understandable." Mist laughed, thinking of the way Clive's face lit up every time he saw Betty. "I think you get distracted easily there."

"Well, what guy wouldn't around two such pretty women."

Mist smiled, set aside the paintings she was leaving with Clive, closed up the tub, and left Clive to finish up the ornament.

* * *

Settled back in the hotel's kitchen, Mist looked over the spread on the kitchen counter, taking in the lush red of the hydrangeas and red berries, the pure, wintery white of the roses, lilies and button mums, and the soothing greens of the cymbidiums, spruce and eucalyptus. The color combination spelled Christmas in every basic traditional way, and the mixture of colors and textures would have been beautiful in simple vases. But Mist's plans always leaned toward the unique. A paper sack sat on one of the kitchen stools, waiting to offer up its contents for Mist's own artistry.

Helena had been a half-day trip for Mist the week before. The city, much larger than Timberton, offered the supplies she desired for this year's holiday decorations. Between antique shops and craft stores, she had found exactly what she needed to make centerpieces for the dining room tables and buffet.

An oblong copper tub had been the most exciting discovery of all. She'd hoped for some type of container that would be a change from the bark-covered pots the year before, as much as she'd been pleased with those. When she'd found a matching set of small copper kettles in a second shop, the designs fell into place. She'd headed straight for a craft store where she picked up several dozen tiny silver bells and metallic gold wire-edged ribbon, a mixed-metal fantasy image in mind.

Now with the copper containers lined up in a row, Mist began to blend the varied flowers into multicolored clusters, weaving gold ribbon in and out of each arrangement, tiny bells peeking out between buds and blossoms. In the end, each small copper kettle held a fantasy burst of blooms, bells, ribbon and cheer, as well as a slender candle. The buffet centerpiece was equally impressive as a larger version. To add to the charm, all it would take was a slight nudge to any of the arrangements to set off an unexpected chime of bells.

Mist stepped back, satisfied with the table decorations. Setting them in the front parlor, she retired to her room. Late evenings were her personal time, and her watercolors waited.

FOUR

Mist already had coffee brewing and banana nut muffins in the oven when Betty entered the kitchen and took a seat at the center counter. From the way the hotelkeeper opened the registration book and hovered over it, Mist knew she was working on logistics of some sort.

"Checking over room assignments?" Mist asked as she poured coffee into the hotelkeeper's favorite holiday mug—a plaid gingerbread-man design—and set the fresh brewed beverage in front of her.

"Something like that," Betty said, running her finger down a list of names.

"We have rooms set for everyone, Betty. Do you think some need to be changed?" Mist took a seat across from her.

Betty sighed. "I don't know. You're better at this than I am."

"I doubt it," Mist said kindly. "You've been doing this much longer than I have."

"Maybe, but you have a way of knowing where people will be most comfortable. You have that... thing, you know, that intuition thing. Tell me what you think of this. I'm not sure how to handle it."

Mist reached out as Betty turned the registration book in her direction. Nothing had been changed, but several post-it notes had been added.

"Belinda Myers needs privacy?" Mist read from one note, seeing that Ms. Myers had been assigned a room near several other guests. "When did this come up?"

"Last night. I didn't want to interrupt your evening time since I know you use it to paint. But I had a phone call from her... manager." Betty sighed.

"Her manager?" Mist repeated. "I don't understand."

"I didn't either at first," Betty said. "Apparently Belinda Myers isn't Belinda Myers."

"I must say you've completely lost me now," Mist admitted. She reached behind her head and removed a carved teakwood hair clip, letting her soft brown hair fall loosely across her shoulders. She then wound her hair back up and clipped it in place again, as if rearranging it would sort out the odd conversation. "Though, really, if you think about it, anyone might be someone else."

The hotelkeeper's silent stare told Mist her philosophy wasn't going to solve the immediate problem. If it was a problem, that is. "So, who is this guest, Betty? Maybe a simple room change to a quieter section of the hotel is all we need to do."

Betty sighed. "It might be a start, but I'm not sure it'll be enough. It turns out Belinda Myers is actually Catherine Ashley Turner."

Mist drew her arms together. She rested her elbows on the table and placed her chin in her hands, fingers curled around each cuff of her Peruvian alpaca sweater.

Aware the pose gave her face a slight resemblance to a chipmunk, she'd always found it a comfortable position for processing information. And this was information, indeed. Even Mist, who hadn't owned a television set or seen a movie since she was a child, knew who Catherine Ashley Turner was. If there was a level of fame beyond superstardom, the actress fell right in line. This could take a little more coordinating than a room change. Or would it?

"I don't see any reason this should be complicated," Mist said finally. "She's just a person, like anyone else." Even as she heard the words leave her mouth, she knew it wasn't that simple. Fame could have a way of affecting people, and even if it didn't, it affected others around them. It might take some maneuvering to keep the holiday festive yet calm. "All right," Mist added, "we may need to watch the townsfolk when they come by, to make sure no one disturbs her. But she may just want a quiet retreat, might curl up with a book in her room. That would make sense, seeing as she booked a solo trip to a small town."

"I would agree with you," Betty said, "except she's not coming alone."

Mist tilted her head, giving one side of her face more of a chipmunk resemblance than the other. "The reservation is for one person."

"Not anymore." Betty sighed. "Her manager is sending her bodyguard along too."

"Her *bodyguard*?" Mist straightened up and furrowed her brow, an unusual sight on the artist-chef who normally floated through life with surreal calm. "I don't understand."

"He wants to make sure she isn't disturbed."

Mist pondered this new information, equally weighing logistics with overall ambiance for the guests and townsfolk who would be spending much of the holiday weekend at the hotel.

"Maybe we should put Ms. Turner in Room 16," Betty suggested. "It's quiet and at the end of the hallway upstairs. That would give her privacy."

Mist shook her head with a movement so slight it was barely perceptible. "Clara Winslow will want that room again. She loved it last year, and I've placed her favorite quilt on that bed."

"Then what do you suggest?" Betty handed her a pencil. Mist regarded the room assignments quietly, as if contemplating a move on a chessboard.

"We'll put Ms. Turner in Room 23 and her... bodyguard... in Room 22," Mist said. "That will work. I hadn't assigned those rooms to anyone, so they're available. I'll just do some quick freshening up to prepare the rooms for guests. Room 23 has that claw foot tub, which Ms. Turner might enjoy."

"You were going to put Michael Blanton in Room 22," Betty pointed out.

Mist felt the same strange sensation she'd felt earlier as she thought about Michael Blanton's arrival but brushed it away. "He'll be fine in Room 11, where the professor from England stayed last year."

"Any other room changes needed that you can see?"

"No," Mist said. "The three sisters will be in downstairs rooms since two of those open together into a large suite. That won't interfere with Room 7, so Hollister can come and go as he wishes."

"And the Philadelphia guests are already settled in Room 12," Betty said. "This will work nicely."

"Yes, nicely indeed." Mist stood, closed the registration book, and handed it back to Betty. "Looks like I have some rearranging to do."

"And I have some baking to plan," Betty said. "The cookie exchange seems to have crept up suddenly. I suppose holiday events always seem like that. One day it's September, and the next day it's suddenly December. At least it seems that way."

"Time is not always linear," Mist replied, smiling as she headed out of the room. "Oh, and Maisie said to tell you she'll bring snickerdoodles to the exchange."

"What a coincidence." Betty laughed. "I happen to know Clayton loves those."

* * *

Mist opened the door to the downstairs closet, the one she considered her secret stockpile of special items. It was her habit to leave a unique item in each guest's room before arrival.

Often it came down to a last-minute decision, some sort of impulse that inspired her as she looked through the assorted knickknacks she'd accumulated over the past year. For returning guests, she was at a slight advantage, having already met them in the past.

For new guests, it became a challenge, almost a game, to figure out what might intrigue a visitor, or even be noticed, for that matter.

Gathering the items was almost as fun as choosing which ones to put in each guest room. She'd seen how, the year before, a wooden puzzle had gone into the room of a family in need of being put back together. She hadn't known the family was broken at the time she chose the puzzle, only that a child would be staying in that room. Thus began her scavenger hunt for a wide range of trinkets to store in the closet. Perhaps, she thought, even having variety on hand would bring in a varied group of guests, as if the objects themselves called out across the miles, beckoning people toward the hotel. Who was to say? There were many things in life that made no sense at first sight, or were thought to serve one purpose, while serving another. Like a simple wooden child's puzzle.

Reaching up to a high shelf, Mist pulled down a large, woven basket that she'd found at the thrift shop earlier that year. Several inches in height and long enough to stretch the entire length of the shelf, the basket served as a perfect container for small items. She set the basket on the closet floor, sat down, and crossed her legs—*sukhasana*, her Yoga teacher in California would say. She interlaced her fingers, raised her arms over her head and stretched, then lowered them and moved the basket into her lap.

Secondhand Sally's had been a gold mine this year, partially because, she suspected, Sally knew Mist often browsed the thrift shop shelves, looking for unusual items to add to her closet collection. Now rummaging through the basket, she recalled the days she found the tiny picture frame with paw prints, the candle with seashells embedded in its side, and the doll-sized apron with a wild print of purple grapes. A matchbook from a Paris hotel had also come from Secondhand Sally's, as well as a tiny salt spoon with the initial *T*. One by one, she lifted out items and observed them, as if each had a personality or a message to give—a spool doll with a red gingham dress, a miniature china birdhouse, a tin toy fire truck, a harmonica in the key of *C*. And perhaps her favorite find of all was a well-worn copy of *The Velveteen Rabbit* with a torn corner on the title page.

If anyone were to ask the common denominator of all the items in her closet, she would have said "whimsy." No one item in itself seemed important, but each had a meaning, whether apparent or not. She never knew what that meaning would be when she picked up an addition to the collection. After all, what spoke to one person might not be the same to another. It was only in the combination of items and guests that reasons came forth. As they soon would again.

FIVE

The front doorbell of the Timberton Hotel had a distinctive ring, one that hinted at tales of days gone by and people long gone. Mist found it a fascinating, though not disturbing, fact that the signal of an arrival carried echoes of the past. She almost expected to open the door sometime to find Meriweather Lewis stopping in for something warm to drink while on his expedition. Or Myrna Loy, who was born in nearby Helena, Montana, perhaps seeking to escape the glamour of Hollywood, as their soon-to-be guest intended to do. There was no knowing who had come and gone from the hotel in years past or from the area before the hotel even existed.

So intrigued was Mist with these thoughts that the doorbell rang three times before she pulled out of her daze and went to answer it. There, on the front steps, was neither an explorer nor a movie star, but dear Clara Winslow, back for another year of Timberton holiday celebrations.

"Ms. Winslow, how delightful to see you!" Mist welcomed the guest with a warm embrace.

"Don't you dare call me anything but 'Clara,' you hear me?" the elderly woman scolded, though never losing a smile while doing so. "How are you, Mist?

I've been looking forward to seeing you. And to your wonderful meals, of course."

Mist smiled. She knew her reputation for cooking went hand in hand with the draw of Betty's cozy lodging accommodations. Adding in decorations and festivities, it made for a perfect holiday guest experience.

"Do I hear Clara Winslow out there?" Betty's voice preceded her entry. Once she stepped through the kitchen door into the front hallway, she met Clara with an exuberant hug. Mist took the guest's luggage and set it at the foot of the stair s as Betty ushered Clara in. "You look wonderful, Clara!" Betty exclaimed as she stepped back.

Mist had to agree. There was a rosy glow to Clara's face that had been absent the year before. This was understandable since that particular visit had been the first Christmas for Clara after her husband's death. Clearly, the past year had helped to ease the pain. In addition, the elderly woman had fond memories of spending Christmas at the hotel the year before, even though she'd been on her own.

"I have you in Room 16 again, if that's all right with you," Mist said. "I know you were comfortable there last year."

"Of course it is," Clara said, smiling. "Such a lovely room, I remember it well—light and airy. How kind of you to remember."

A phone ringing sent Betty scurrying to the kitchen. "Don't worry about the registration card, Clara. We can fill it out later. Just get yourself settled in and relaxed. Mist will help you." With that the hotelkeeper disappeared, and soon the ringing of the phone ceased. Betty's calm, professional tone told Mist the call was likely business—a guest calling to give an approximate arrival time, for example, or with a request for directions.

Mist escorted Clara to her room and was pleased to see the woman smile at the sight of the Christmas quilt spread across the bed."

"Oh, how I love this quilt! I have to admit I hoped it would be here this time."

"Of course it's here, Clara. This is your home away from home." Mist offered. "We want you to be as comfortable as possible. I'll let you settle in. I'll be downstairs if you need anything. There's coffee and tea in the front parlor, as well as some treats."

"Such as those wonderful glazed cinnamon nuts that Betty makes?"

"Of course," Mist said. "An unlimited supply, as always. Help yourself."

Mist left Clara to get situated and returned downstairs just in time to hear the doorbell again. She walked straight to the door, opened it, and found three women lined up in a row, all of similar height and build. In fact—was she imagining it?—they were identical, other than clothing and hairstyles. No, she wasn't imagining it. The three women were triplets, rare as that was. Mist estimated them to be in their sixties.

"You must be the Anders sisters," Mist said, stepping aside to usher them in.

"Yes," the first one who entered said. She sported a bright red wool scarf. "Like the Andrews Sisters, but not nearly as musical." The woman laughed, as did the one who stepped in behind her, a green knit cap covering her ears and most of her forehead. The third had neither a scarf nor hat on but wore blue mittens with a faux fur trim. She remained silent, sighing as if tired of what was likely a long-running joke.

"Welcome to the Timberton Hotel," Mist said. "Let me take your coats and winter accessories. How was your trip?"

"Trips," the third, more serious sister, clarified as she removed her coat and hung it on a coatrack herself.

"Yes, of course," Mist said. "I hope you *each* had a pleasant trip. You all live in different parts of the country, I believe." Small talk ranked low as a preferred mode of communication for Mist, but she sensed a tension between the sisters. If not the first two who had entered, then definitely the third. A little chatter might help lighten the mood.

"That's right," the sister with the bright red scarf said. "I'm Lydia, from Charleston, and this is Helen, from Seattle." The second sister smiled but remained quiet.

"And I'm Deirdre," the third sister said.

"From Boston," Lydia added.

"Yes," Mist said. "Well, we're glad you all made it safe and sound. I have registration cards for you to fill out, and then I'll show you to your rooms. Help yourselves to some coffee or tea and glazed cinnamon walnuts over on the buffet."

"Don't mind if I do!" The clearly masculine voice caused all four women to turn in the direction of the kitchen, where Clive leaned against the doorway.

"And who is this handsome man?" Lydia flashed a smile as flirtatious as her words.

Mist wasn't certain if she was humored or concerned by the grin that spread across Clive's face. She could hear Betty still on the phone in the kitchen, likely not overhearing the current banter.

"Clive Barnes at your service, ma'am, er... ma'ams, that is," he said as he looked past Lydia and around at the other sisters. He let out a soft whistle. Mist smiled, in spite of herself. Clive wasn't known for subtlety. He'd clearly noticed the similarity between the three women. "It would be my pleasure to help you with your bags."

"That would be appreciated," Deirdre said.

It took merely a few minutes to show the sisters to their accommodations, Lydia and Helen choosing the rooms with a connecting door, Deirdre taking the third room. Clive delivered the luggage to each room and returned to the kitchen. Mist followed shortly behind.

"Everyone getting settled in?" Betty asked. The aroma of cinnamon floated in the air as Betty arranged glazed cinnamon nuts on wax paper to cool.

"As settled as possible," Mist said. "I sense some sisterly tension, at least on the part of one sister. We'll see if a bit of holiday ambiance can give her some peace."

"If anyone can make that happen, it's you," Betty said.

"We can only help," Mist pointed out. "Peace comes from within. It's up to each person to find it. With three sisters… they may need to help each other. We'll see." Mist paused. "Yes, we'll see."

"Meanwhile, we have two guests yet to arrive," Betty said.

"Actually, three," Mist said.

"That's right," Betty said. "Counting Ms. Turner's bodyguard."

Clive set his coffee mug down on the counter and looked at Betty. "I could swear you just said bodyguard, but I haven't had my hearing checked recently."

"Nothing wrong with your hearing, Clive," Betty said.

"We have a guest arriving with a bodyguard," Mist explained. "Though I find the concept of a bodyguard disconcerting, really. To have a wall between a person and the experience of life seems unfortunate."

"Unfortunate but maybe necessary," Betty said.

"Anyone want to clue me in?" Clive's expression was a mixture of amused and perplexed. "This is beginning to sound complicated."

"It's not at all complicated," Mist said. "It turns out one of our guests is a celebrity with a protective manager who felt a bodyguard should come along on the trip."

"The guest is Catherine Ashley Turner," Betty said.

"Cat?" Clive's eyebrows lifted. "You mean *the* Cat?"

"Yes, Clive," Betty said. "That's exactly who we mean."

"And you didn't tell me?"

"We didn't know," Betty said. "She was registered as Belinda Myers. Her manager only called this morning. And I don't think they want it to be big news. The whole point of using a different name was to avoid that."

"When is she due to arrive?" Mist asked the question merely as a matter of conversation. She knew all the guests would be in by the evening.

"Soon," Betty said. "That phone call was her manager. They should be arriving within the hour."

"Can't the woman even make her own phone calls?" Clive asked.

"I'm sure she can," Betty said. "She's probably simply in the habit of letting others handle arrangements."

"I think that would be difficult," Mist mused.

"Difficult?" Clive laughed. "Sounds easy enough to me."

Mist shook her head. "Having help might seem easy at first, but I suspect a loss of independence could make a person weary as time goes on."

"Well, I do believe this will be an interesting weekend," Betty said.

"I suspect you're right," Mist said. "In fact, I have no doubt."

SIX

Mist returned to the kitchen, satisfied that a quick room check had confirmed the guest rooms were ready for the remaining arrivals. Betty was placing a tray of flourless peanut butter chocolate chip cookies in the oven when the doorbell rang. Without hesitation, Mist went to answer the door, glad that Clive had returned to his gallery. The less fuss Ms. Turner's arrival brought on, the better.

Whatever Mist had expected when she opened the door, she was surprised. Cat looked nothing like the few photos she'd seen of her. The world-famous star sported a basic winter beanie pulled low over her ears, sunglasses, and a plain coat that could have been from a thrift store—or belonged in one. Her legendary blond curls straggled out from an army-green cable-knit cap in straight strands. She wore no makeup, as far as Mist could tell, though what appeared to be diamond studs of ample size peeked out just below the edge of her cap. A man of short height and slim frame stood quietly behind and to the left of the celebrity, holding two overnight bags, presumably one for each of them.

"Welcome to the Timberton Hotel," Mist said, stepping back. With a gentle sweep of her arm, she ushered the newcomers in. "We're delighted to have you staying with us, Ms. Turner and..." She left the sentence open-ended, unsure of the other person's name. Could this be the bodyguard Betty had told her to expect? His small stature hardly fit her preconceived image, though she chastised herself immediately for stereotyping, something she'd always felt was a weakness.

"Simon," the man said, his voice unassuming, though not quite weak. He nodded formally, in a polite manner, but didn't lower a bag to extend his arm for a handshake. "Charming little place," he added.

"Thank you," Mist replied. "We love it, and we enjoy sharing it with our guests. I'm sure you'll enjoy spending your holidays here. The atmosphere is festive but peaceful."

"That sounds perfect." The first words spoken by the woman were soft and, if Mist interpreted their tone correctly, relieved. "Festive but peaceful," she repeated as if the thought itself was a Christmas gift. Mist suspected that was exactly what it was to this particular guest.

"Let's get you settled in," Mist said, closing the front door. "We have registration cards over on the front counter for you to sign, and then I'll show you to your rooms, Ms. Turner and Mr. Simon."

"It's just Simon," the man said. He approached the counter, picked up a pen, and began filling out the required information.

"And please just call me Cathy," the woman added, a wistful smile appearing on her face.

"Very well," Mist agreed. "And you may call me Mist."

"Mist," Cathy said, contemplating the unusual name. "How lovely."

Once again, Mist was struck by the woman's countenance. Nothing about her hinted at celebrity or fame.

The sound of the kitchen door swinging open signaled Betty's entrance. Mist smiled at the sight of the hotelkeeper, whose poinsettia-print apron was covered with flour.

"I heard conversation and wanted to say hello," Betty said. "We're delighted to have you staying with us for the Christmas holiday. You're in good hands with Mist." She paused, and then laughed, aware of her appearance. "Cookies. I've been baking for an event tomorrow."

"Ah." Cathy's tone brightened considerably. "Are you having an old-fashioned cookie exchange? We used to have those when I was growing up in Michigan. They were so much fun."

"Yes," Betty said. "We have one every year. It's a Timberton Hotel tradition."

"Well, I would have come here for that alone," Cathy said. "I used to make pecan shortbread for ours. Even won a contest with that recipe one year."

"Really?" Betty exclaimed. "That's fabulous. We don't have a contest here, but we do have fun testing all the goods at this time of year. You're certainly welcome to join in. Speaking of which, I'd better get back to work, or we won't have peanut butter cookies in the mix." Betty disappeared back into the kitchen, a slight trail of flour floating behind her.

Simon finished filling out the registration cards and returned to the luggage.

"Let me help you with those," Mist offered, only to be politely refused.

"Just directions to our rooms will be fine," he said.

"Of course. I have your rooms ready," Mist said, lifting two keys from behind the counter. "Follow me." She headed up the stairway, both new guests behind her. Aiming for the far end of the upstairs hallway, she arrived at Rooms 22 and 23. "Your manager called and requested privacy," Mist explained. "I think you'll be very comfortable here."

"Marty is always too concerned," Cathy said. "Any rooms would have been fine. But thank you for your consideration."

"Well, I do hope you'll feel comfortable joining in with some of our holiday activities," Mist said. "That's entirely up to you, of course. Let me know if there's anything I can do to help make your stay pleasant and relaxing." She unlocked each room and handed a key to each guest, pointing out linens, light switches, and amenities. Leaving them to settle in, she returned to the kitchen, where Betty's apron had now doubled its flour arsenal.

"She seems quite nice," Betty said, pressing a fork into the top of each round ball of dough on a baking sheet."

"Yes, I agree," Mist said. "The gentleman is quiet, but perhaps he's tired from the trip."

"I suppose that's her bodyguard? We aren't expecting anyone else to show up with Ms. Turner. Her manager said two people total. He just seemed... not what I would expect."

"I had the same reaction," Mist admitted. "But I think we have a movie version in our heads of what bodyguards look like."

"Maybe," Betty agreed. "But I still might prefer Arnold Schwarzenegger or Vin Diesel around if someone tried to attack me."

"Is that so?" Both Betty and Mist jumped at the sound of Clive's voice but relaxed when they saw him grinning.

"Unless Clive Barnes happened to be there, of course," Betty added quickly.

Clive laughed. "I take it the celebrity guest has arrived."

"Yes," Mist said. "And she's nothing like what you are probably expecting. I have a feeling she's just hoping for a quiet holiday away from the hectic lifestyle she has."

Betty nodded. "I agree. So you behave yourself around her, Clive Barnes."

Clive furrowed his brow. "I'll consider it... if you let me test one of those cookies. I could smell them halfway between the gallery and here."

"What do you think, Mist?" Betty said. "Is our guest's comfort worth the price of a cookie?"

"Maybe two cookies," Clive interjected, thinking the situation over. "In fact, how many guests will you have this weekend?"

"You're pushing your luck, my dear man," Betty said, smiling as she removed one tray of cookies from the oven and placed another inside. "But if you let these cool a few minutes, you can test this batch."

"That's my girl," Clive said, moving over to Betty and placing a soft kiss on her forehead. "So all your guests have arrived?"

"All but one," Betty said. "Michael Blanton should be here within the next few hours. I forgot to tell you, Mist. He called earlier to say his plane had landed in Bozeman, but he planned to run some errands before driving out here."

"It will be nice to have everyone here," Mist said casually. "I should go double-check the front parlor, hotel entrance, and café to make sure everything is ready." She grabbed a container of glazed cinnamon walnuts and stepped out of the room, quite sure she saw Betty and Clive exchange grins as she left the kitchen.

SEVEN

Silver tinsel tickled Mist's face as she reached to straighten the front parlor curtains. The heat flowing upward from floor vents gave the Christmas tree an illusion of life. It only took a close stance to the evergreen branches to feel an ornament tap a shoulder or a strand of garland brush against an arm.

Evening had settled over the hotel, warm and comforting, quiet and peaceful. Though the following day promised energy and activity, the day that was ending had been low-key, with guests arriving, the aroma of cookies baking, a wine-and-cheese hour that had brought a few people out to mingle, and now a silent building. Close to ten p.m. already, Betty had long retired to her private quarters, just as guests had settled in for the night. Mist had served a simple dinner in the café, knowing townsfolk would be saving their appetites for the Christmas Eve feast. Clean-up from the meal took little time, as did refilling the glazed cinnamon nuts bowl and placing cookies out for late-night snacks. Mist had changed from work clothes into a soft burgundy dress with gold embroidery and clipped her hair back with a carved wooden barrette. The long day had still left a good hour for Mist to paint, keeping the door to her room open in order to hear the doorbell.

Now, standing in the front parlor, Mist glanced at the quiet street as she pulled the curtains together. The last remaining guest had yet to arrive, in spite of the late hour. Although snow was forecast for the following day, the evening was clear and driving conditions were favorable. Perhaps Betty had misunderstood Michael Blanton's earlier phone call. Had he said he would be arriving the following day instead? No, she was certain he was only detained for errands and would still be at the hotel that evening.

Mist settled into an armchair to wait, letting the rayon fabric drape softly against her legs. She browsed the stack of books she'd chosen earlier for the side table. *The Canterbury Tales, Walden, David Copperfield, The Call of the Wild, On the Road.*

When a beam of headlights finally filtered through the curtains, announcing the arrival of the last guest, Mist sighed, a mix of relief, fatigue, and anticipation. She moved to the front hallway and listened as a car door opened and closed. Then, at the sound of footsteps on the porch, she opened the door.

"Mist." Michael Blanton smiled, his brown hair tussled from the wind, a wool neck scarf in shades of forest green and mustard gold accentuating his unusual eyes.

"Mr. Blanton."

"You're not going to insist on calling me Mr. Blanton, are you?" Michael stepped into the lobby as Mist moved aside to usher him in.

"Michael," she rephrased.

"Much better." Michael set a suitcase down and removed his scarf and coat, hanging them on the coatrack in the corner of the room. As he crossed the foyer, Mist noted with relief that his limp from the previous year's visit was gone.

"I've been looking forward to being here this year," Michael continued. "And to visiting with you. I was delighted when Betty told me you were still here."

"I will always be here even if I'm not," Mist said. "I don't think we ever completely leave a place after we grow fond of it."

"I agree," Michael replied, smiling. "This is why I come back here every holiday season. Christmas at the Timberton Hotel has a special place in my heart." He followed Mist to the counter, filled out the registration card, and took a room key from Mist's outstretched hand.

"Room 11, at the top of the stairs," Mist said. "It's not the room you had last time, but we have more guests and needed to do some shuffling. I hope it will be satisfactory."

"Ah, the room the English professor stayed in last year. He was quite a character." Michael laughed. "Will he be returning this year?"

"Not this year," Mist said. "Perhaps next year though. We received a Christmas card from him last week, saying he looked forward to bringing his family here in the future. Clara Winslow is back again though."

"Yes, we keep in touch during the year. I'm looking forward to seeing her, as well as enjoying Timberton again. This is such a beautiful town—perfect for a winter holiday, so peaceful with the snow, so invigorating with crisp night air."

"It's a beautiful town any time of the year," Mist said. "The snow is calming, but spring brings a burst of color in every garden. Summer offers a soft, warm afternoon breeze. Every season has its own charm."

"Yes, I can imagine that's the case." Michael picked up his suitcase and started for the stairs. "I can't wait to relax in that front parlor chair, though I suspect sleep will catch up with me tonight."

"You'll find plenty of choices for reading on the side table, whether tonight or tomorrow. I'm about to turn in, but I'll see you at breakfast."

"Thank you." Michael paused at the foot of the stairs. "It's great to see you, Mist."

"And you," Mist said.

* * *

Late morning sunlight filled the hotel kitchen. Mist found Betty sipping a mug of coffee, Clara Winslow beside her, dropping snowball cookies onto a baking sheet.

"Everyone seems to have settled in," Betty said. "Especially Clara here, who, as you can see, has insisted on contributing to the cookie exchange."

"How delightful and kind of you to contribute as well," Mist said.

"Nothing kind about it." Clara laughed. "You're giving me far too much credit. I'm just after a tray of mixed cookies at the end, like everyone else."

"For a special friend back home," Betty whispered, her voice purposely loud enough to make sure Clara overheard.

"Is that so?" Mist looked at Clara, pleasantly surprised.

"Now, now, girls, don't make too much of it," Clara said, avoiding eye contact. "They're just for a nice gentleman from my church group who's been kind enough to give me rides home from church several times."

"Well, I'd say he deserves a batch of cookies," Mist said, not missing a light flush on Clara's face.

"My thoughts exactly," Betty said cheerfully. She and Mist exchanged knowing glances, each pleased that Clara was being social. It was time, now that she'd been a widow for over a year. She deserved to be happy.

"Indeed," Mist said before changing the subject. "The hotel has been quiet. Guests seem content to just relax for now."

"That's not surprising," Betty said. "Traveling is tiring. Breakfast was simple and casual too, which was nice."

"Yes," Mist agreed. "Clayton's crew came through early, as always, but without Clayton, which surprised Maisie when she stopped in. A few other locals stopped by too."

"I shared a table with Michael," Clara piped up. "It was great catching up. He's doing so well, don't you think?

"Absolutely," Mist said. "I was delighted to see the two of you chatting."

"I noticed two of the Anders sisters sat together," Betty said. "But the third sister skipped the meal, had a mug of coffee by herself in the front room."

"I noticed that too," Mist said. "And Ms. Turner and Simon asked for trays to be brought up to their rooms, which I delivered, along with a tray for Hollister, downstairs. I believe the Callahans took some apple-cinnamon muffins to go and left to take a drive through the countryside."

"Yes, I filled a thermos of coffee for them to take along. It's a perfect day for a drive, that's for sure," Betty pointed out. "What with the sun shining and the roads clear. Hardly seems like December, other than the light blanket of snow on the ground from last week. I do hope we get some new snowfall for Christmas. It would be nice for the guests to see it coming down. There's something special about a white Christmas."

"Like being inside a snow globe," Mist said.

"Or looking into one," Betty added. "It's warmer to watch from inside the hotel."

"But then you miss the soft brush of snowflakes against your face," Mist said. "I love that feeling of a cool whisper against skin."

"I'll check the weather report," Betty said. "Last time I looked, it didn't show snow coming until next week."

"The weather has its own timetable, not one always shared in advance." Mist smiled as if this were a secret, though she knew it should be common knowledge to anyone. "How's the cookie exchange shaping up? Clara's batch looks like a great addition."

"Why thank you, Mist," Clara said.

A proud smile crept across Betty's face. "Should be the best one yet. You know I told all the girls they could add a few different items this year—within reason, of course. It *is* a cookie exchange, after all."

Mist nodded. "Maisie's bringing snickerdoodles, as you know. And I think Marge is bringing divinity puffs. She was excited to have other options included in the event."

"We'll still have many of the standards," Betty said. "People count on those."

The kitchen door cracked open, and Michael stuck his head in to say hello.

"Why, Michael Blanton, look at you!" Betty crossed the floor and opened the door the rest of the way, pulling Michael into the room, as well as into a sincere embrace. "We're so happy to have you back again this year. Clara tells us you're doing well. We were just chatting about you."

"In full remission," Michael said. "I'm very grateful."

Mist let out a silent sigh of relief. She'd watched his casual walk across the foyer earlier and noticed the absence of the limp he'd had the prior year after surgery to remove a tumor from his leg. This confirmed her hopes that his easy walk across the lobby to the staircase earlier had been a good sign.

"Help yourself," Betty said, pointing to the tray of cookies.

"Thank you, Betty," Michael said. "I think I'll wait. I'm still full from that delicious frittata Mist served for breakfast. I'm going to grab a cup of coffee and sit in the front room to read. It seems I've been given quite the reading assignment for the weekend." He directed the comment to Mist, delivering it with a wink.

Mist smiled as she casually looked away, busying herself by unfolding and refolding a kitchen towel. "You know those are just a few choices. There are more books in the shelf by the fireplace, as well. And let me check the coffee and tea service in the entryway. We like to keep that available to guests all day."

"The coffee and tea are fine, don't worry," Betty said. "I refilled the cream and sugar too. You might check the fire. I haven't thrown a log on it for a while. Clive split some wood for us the other day. If you need more, you'll find it out back."

"No need." Clive's voice called from the front hallway. "I just filled the metal rack beside the fireplace and threw a new log on to get the fire going again." He stepped into the kitchen, shook Michael's hand in greeting, and grabbed a cookie before Betty had a chance to either offer one or stop him.

"What brings you up here at this time of day?" Betty asked. "Isn't the gallery open today?"

"It is." Clive nodded. "And that's why I'm here." He turned to Mist. "There are some customers asking about your paintings."

"The ones I delivered yesterday?" Mist raised one eyebrow slightly.

"Not exactly," Clive said. "I think you might want to talk to them. They seem to be looking for something in particular."

Mist placed the folded towel on a rack and turned toward Clive. "Of course I'll be happy to come down to the gallery. Give me a few minutes, and I'll meet you there."

"Thanks, Mist," Clive said. "And don't rush. They went over to Marge's to pick up some of her homemade fudge. I think they'll be stuck there for a bit once they see her selection."

Betty laughed. "That wouldn't surprise me at all. I didn't even know there could be so many varieties of fudge before I met Marge—mint chocolate, cherry almond, butterscotch, raspberry, peanut butter honey, maple walnut, vanilla coconut, white chocolate pecan and, of course, the best of all: caramel. That one counter she has just for fudge goes on and on."

"Well, now you've got my sweet tooth revved up," Michael said. "Maybe I will take one of those cookies after all."

"That's a good idea," Betty said, pulling a small plate out of a cupboard and stacking up a generous portion of cookies. "You just put those by that armchair you like to read in. If you don't eat the others, someone will."

"I can guarantee that," Clive said.

"Another *guest*," Betty clarified, wrinkling her nose at Clive.

"I can take a hint." Clive raised his hands as he scooted out the back kitchen door, laughing.

"I'll grab a book and claim my favorite chair," Michael said. He thanked Betty for the cookies and left.

"And I'm full steam ahead on baking cookies." Betty scraped another spoonful of batter from her mixing bowl and went back to work.

"All right then," Mist said. "It sounds like we all have our plans for this morning. And I have dinner to prepare later on too, so I'd better head over to the gallery."

EIGHT

A brisk wind blew leaves along the sidewalk as Mist walked to the gallery. She pulled the turtleneck of her sweater up over her chin and slipped her mitten-clad hands into her coat pockets. Scattered clouds dotted the sky, none heavy enough to hint at snow. Still, the temperature left no doubt that it was winter. The wind chill factor had to be in the teens.

Clive opened the gallery door as Mist approached— an unusual gesture that raised both her eyebrows and her curiosity. Even more surprising, he closed the door as soon as she stepped in, turning the "open" side over to "closed."

"Clive?" Mist asked, not getting an answer. Instead, she followed the direction of his extended arm, toward the center of the room. There she found Ms. Turner and Simon—or was it Mr. Simon?— standing at a worktable, looking at several of Mist's miniature paintings in a row. Several other small canvases sat to the side, all Mist's. Ms. Turner took one from the side and added it to the arrangement of others and then picked up another and did the same. She switched the order of the canvases around, comparing the different designs in relation to each other. Mist pulled off her mittens and put them in her pockets, then approached and stood beside Ms. Turner, taking in the same overview. After some contemplation, she reached out and moved one square to a different location, earning a cautious glance from Simon, who reached out to move it back.

"No, she's right, it's better there." Ms. Turner held her hand up and then smiled, looking over the arrangement. "These are beautiful, Mist. I love the soft textures and mix of colors. It's as if there's a mountain stream running through them, tying them together. Maybe it's the light brushstrokes. They remind me of water."

"Do you paint, Ms. Turner?" Mist asked.

"Please, you must call me Cat. In fact, Cathy would be wonderful. I'm so tired…" Her voice trailed off. "Anyway, no, I don't paint. I used to. I… well, it isn't important now." She shifted her position, looking over the canvas arrangement again.

"You miss it," Mist said softly.

"I haven't thought about it for a long time," Cathy said. "But now looking at your wonderful paintings, I realize I do."

"Ms. Turner would like to order more, Mist." Clive spoke up, not one to miss a sales opportunity.

"It's Cathy," both Mist and Cathy said at the same time.

"I'd be delighted to make more up for you," Mist offered. "I could have a few done within the next couple of days, before you leave."

"I believe that won't be enough time," Clive said, a slight cough making its way into his statement, as if a speck of dust caught in his throat.

"Well, you let me know what you'd like, and I'll put it together for you," Mist said.

Cathy turned to Simon, diamond earrings catching the gallery lights, a stark contrast to her casual jeans and sweatshirt. "How large is our living room wall?"

Our wall. Mist caught the comment without reacting.

"I'll call the architect and find out." Simon pulled out a cell phone and dialed. "I'd guess the open space is about thirty feet wide," he added while waiting for the line to connect.

"And how high is your ceiling?" Clive's voice still sounded rough. Or was he nervous? Mist pondered his odd behavior. Was he starstruck? Was he simply hoping for a good sale? Clive was well-known for his reputation as a smooth salesperson.

"Eighteen feet." Cathy sighed, as if the height of the wall were more of a downside than a plus, as many would consider it.

"Thirty by eighteen," Mist mused, the dimensions forming in her mind. "And what is the color of the paint?"

"The paint?" Clive scratched his chin, confused.

"Yes, the paint on the wall," Mist said, answering Clive and then turning to Cathy. "If you would like a few paintings on the wall, the background color is important."

"It can be any color you'd like," Cathy said. "Whatever you think is best."

"I see." A fluid vision of the wall formed in Mist's mind, a spatial expanse of changing images, colors and tones. *A golden sunset. The sky on a starless night. Warm sand along the gulf shoreline.*

"Twenty-eight feet," Simon said, sliding his cell phone into his jacket.

"That was fast," Cathy commented.

"They had the blueprints out already," Simon explained, "to work on the changes to the north wing."

Cathy sighed. "It's so unnecessary, the extra wing. Why can't... Oh, it doesn't matter." She turned toward Mist. "What color would you paint the wall?"

"For a background to art, I prefer neutral—off-white or a pale ivory but without much yellow," Mist said. "Something subtle enough to showcase whatever other art you bring in."

"There won't be any other art on this wall," Clive said.

"Oh," Mist said, uncertain what her next words should be. She looked at Clive, noting a smile had replaced his earlier tentative expression, and then looked at Cathy. "Well, then what portion of that space would you like to use for these paintings?"

"All of it," Cathy said.

"All of it," Mist repeated, just to make sure she had heard correctly. "Twenty-eight by eighteen feet..."

"Yes." Cathy rearranged the small paintings again, experimenting with the spacing before turning back to Mist. "How much room do you think we should leave between each one?"

Mist closed her eyes, attempting to picture the spacious wall, and then opened them. "Do you prefer solid ground or air?"

"We just need measurements, I think," Simon said hesitantly. "Right, Clive?" Both men shrugged their shoulders.

"No, wait." Cathy looked back at Mist. "I understand the question. I prefer air."

"I would choose the same thing," Mist agreed, "for a sensation of floating, for peace of mind, for lightness of spirit."

"Perfect." Cathy smiled.

"Are there particular images you'd like?" Clive picked up a form for special orders and began to fill it out.

Cathy paused, thinking, and then looked at Mist. "Everything."

Clive stopped writing. "Everything?"

"Yes, Clive," Mist said, a slow smile spreading across her face. "You don't need to write out any details. I know what Cathy wants."

* * *

"What was the mystery about?" Betty asked as Mist stepped in through the back door. "I've never seen Clive act so strangely about a sale."

"It's an unusual order," Mist said casually. "I don't think he was sure how to handle it."

"Something out of the ordinary? Or a difficult customer?" Betty took a final batch of snowball cookies out of the oven and turned the oven off. She set the tray aside to cool and looked over the wide spread of cookies covering the counter, some already boxed in containers. "There. I told Clara I'd pull out the last batch for her. That should do it for the cookie exchange tomorrow." She rubbed her hands together in satisfaction and wiped them against a holly-patterned apron.

"Yes, the order at the gallery is wonderfully out of the ordinary," Mist said, "but not a difficult customer at all. "In fact, the customer is Ms. Turner."

"Really?" Betty exclaimed. "Our Ms. Turner from here? Cat?"

"She prefers to be called Cathy, it turns out."

"I like that name," Betty said. "Nice, simple, old-fashioned—nothing that shouts stardom."

"I have a feeling that's why she likes it. I sense she's missing freedom, space, ordinary life. We all need air to breathe. And water..." Mist paused, remembering Cathy's initial comments about the paintings.

"Yes," Betty said as she stacked containers of cookies and moved them aside, ready for the next day's event. "I suppose when it comes right down to it, we all need the same things."

The sound of the telephone ringing sent both Betty and Mist scurrying toward the front reception desk. Betty reached the phone first, greeting the caller and then opening the reservation book, flipping forward to June. Mist smiled. Advance reservations were always a good sign.

Leaving Betty to handle business, Mist continued to the front parlor where, as she expected, Michael sat in the armchair by the fireplace, a book in his hands. Dressed in corduroy slacks, an argyle sweater, and loafers, he looked more like a preppy college student than a man on vacation. The look suited him though, and Mist found herself fighting back a smile.

"Which one did you choose?" Mist leaned sideways, a strand of seashells sliding past her shoulder as she attempted to read the cover. "Ah, *The Call of The Wild.* One of my favorites. It's not your first time reading it, I bet."

Michael smiled. "No, probably my fourth or fifth. But it's been a few years. Reading it again reminds me how intriguing the concept of destiny is." He slipped a bookmark into the spine and closed the book, setting it aside. "How much of what happens to us in life is free will, and how much is fate?"

Though phrased as a question, Mist knew the words were meant to be rhetorical. There was no perfect answer, and they both knew it. Jack London's main character, Buck, had to adapt to a series of harrowing circumstances. In the end, did he face the future as a result of his experiences, or did he merely follow preordained instincts set long before he was born?

"It's a good question," Mist said, sitting down on a couch across from Michael. She crossed one leg over the other, displaying work boots that formed an odd contrast to her sage-colored, distressed silk skirt, a favorite find at Secondhand Sally's. "One without a perfect answer."

"But it's something to think about, isn't it?" Michael leaned forward, clasped his hands together, and rested his elbows on his knees.

A third voice entered the conversation. "Maybe we end up where we are because we follow what others tell us to do, rather than making our own choices." Cathy crossed the room and took a place on the couch beside Mist. Her diamond earrings had been replaced with simple silver hoops, and her hair was pulled back and held with a black elastic band. With her face scrubbed clean of makeup, she could have fit in unnoticed almost anywhere.

Michael shifted in his chair, a spark of recognition in his eyes. He stood and extended an arm, introducing himself. "Michael Blanton," he said. Mist was pleased, though not at all surprised, to see him sit back, relaxed again, undaunted by the presence of a celebrity.

"Cathy Turner, pleased to meet you."

"We're still choosing," Mist said, as much to herself as to anyone else. "Maybe not even considering that we could say no."

"I think about that often," Cathy said. "Many decisions are made for me. I go along with them, and sometimes I have to. But now that I have a few days to reflect, I think I could say 'no' more often than I do. Like the new house, for example."

"The one you're having built," Mist said.

"Yes, the one I'm... Actually, there's an example, probably an extreme one. That house is not going to be just for me. Simon and I are building it together, as a home."

Mist nodded, remembering the "our wall" comment at the gallery. "I suspected as much."

"Ah, so he's not a bodyguard," Michael said.

Cathy laughed. "Oh, yes he is. I wouldn't try to tackle him. He's a former Navy Seal, as well as a black belt in karate. We grew closer after working together." She paused. "The powers that be decided it would be best to keep my status as single and available. But I'm tired of others deciding how I should live my life outside of work. Or, rather, how I should make it appear."

"I can't imagine how difficult that would be," Michael said.

"And exhausting," Mist added softly.

"Yes, that's it exactly!" Cathy exhaled and relaxed against the couch. "I've never thought of it that way before. But it *is* exhausting, always watching what I say, how I appear in public." Turning the conversation in a lighter direction, Cathy addressed Michael. "Mist and I have been talking about art. She's agreed to create a set of paintings for me. And Simon," she added, smiling.

"How wonderful," Michael said. "She's a talented artist. You won't be disappointed. I have one painting of hers that I keep on a wall at home. I enjoy seeing it every day."

Mist felt herself blush at the praise. She'd had many compliments on her art over the years, yet the thought of Michael seeing on a daily basis the painting she'd given him the Christmas before came as a surprise.

"Any particular subject matter for the new paintings?" Michael asked.

Mist straightened her skirt, uncrossing her legs and placing her work boots quietly on the floor. She glanced at Cathy and then back at Michael. "Yes, everything."

"Everything?"

"Everything under the sun," Cathy said. "She can surprise me."

Michael smiled. "I'm sure she will. How many paintings are we talking about?"

Mist and Cathy looked at each other and then back at Michael.

"No more than two hundred, I think," Cathy said. "Based on the size of the wall."

"That sounds about right," Mist said casually. She almost felt guilty being pleased at the stunned look on Michael's face.

Sharp pounding on the front door interrupted the discussion.

"More guests arriving?" Michael asked.

Mist shook her head. "No, everyone has already checked in."

"Locals then," Cathy offered. Mist noted a trace of wishful thinking in the statement.

"They wouldn't knock. Locals come and go during business hours, for meals at Moonglow, or just to have coffee and visit. I'll see who it is," Mist said, standing. Noticing Cathy's uncomfortable expression, she was prepared when she opened the door.

Scruffy, anxious, and practically hyperventilating described the two men who stood on the doorstep of the hotel. Cameras hung haphazardly across winter jackets not quite zipped up, as if they'd been thrown on in a hurry while scrambling into their vehicle. One of the men looked weathered, pushing midfifties. The other, barely into his twenties, had an eager expression halfway between charming and obnoxious.

"Can I help you gentlemen?" Mist looked the two over, waiting for the obvious question.

"We only want some photos, miss, and we'll be on our way," the older man said.

Mist raised one arm, pointing behind them. "The town square is especially lovely today. I recommend some shots from a northern angle. There's just enough snow on the ground to catch the sunlight."

Not dissuaded, the men didn't even bother to follow the direction of her arm.

"Don't play coy with us. We know she's here." This came from the younger man, who balanced on tiptoes, trying to look over Mist's shoulder.

"I'm sorry, are you looking for anyone in particular?" Mist cocked her head to the side, assuming a puzzled air.

Both men paused, appearing to second-guess their location. The younger one adjusted the camera strap around his neck and spoke up. "We have a tip that there's someone special here."

"Yes, you're right." Mist straightened her head and nodded as both men grew excited. She paused, simply for her own impish pleasure. "In fact, there are many special people here. All our guests are special. Just like you two are special."

The older man huffed. "We're talking *extra* special, if you get my drift."

"Well, yes, now that you mention it," Mist said. "Every person here is *extra* special. I believe my comment before didn't adequately describe the human spirit."

"You know exactly what we're talking about," the younger man insisted. "We heard Cat was staying in Timberton. Since this is the only hotel, she must be here." As Mist observed, half-amused, half-stunned, the young man actually meowed, which earned him a bizarre glare from his fellow photographer.

"I'm afraid you're mistaken," Mist said. "We have only a few guests, and they are all ordinary people. Everyday people, just like you two guys, just like me."

"No one *extra* special?" the younger man said, clearly disappointed.

"No one more special than anyone else."

"Then we apologize for bothering you, miss," the older man said.

"It's quite all right," Mist said. She closed the door, rolled her head from one side to the other, squared her shoulders, and smiled.

NINE

As Mist added a dish of toasted sweet corn pudding to the dinner buffet and arranged the basket and sign for customers to "pay what your heart tells you," her own unique philosophy of restaurant pricing, a chattering of voices accompanied the sound of the front door opening and closing.

"Why do we have to go through this every year?" a female voice said. "Every Christmas, for that matter?"

"Because that's when it happened, of course," a second, equally exuberant, female voice replied. "When the holidays roll around, I'm reminded, that's all."

"As if I'm not since I have to hear about it all over again every Christmas," a third voice chimed in.

Mist peeked around the corner, observing all three Anders sisters hovered together just inside the entry. It was difficult to tell who was the most perturbed, but if Mist had to guess, she would put Deirdre, the aloof one from Boston, at the head of the line, with Lydia, red scarf and all, second, and Helen, the third, doing the softer protesting about having to endure whatever was being repeated on a yearly basis.

"It was supposed to be me," Deirdre said, her tone accusatory.

"You were sick!" Lydia exclaimed.

"I should have just cancelled," Deirdre said.

"Well, you agreed." Lydia huffed. "So don't blame me, especially after all this time."

"Every year…" Helen sighed, pulling off her winter gloves. "Every single year…"

Mist felt movement and turned to see Betty behind her, a basket of dinner rolls in one hand and a serving dish with butter in the other.

"What's going on?" Betty whispered.

"Some sort of sisterly sibling disagreement," Mist said, her tone hushed. "Or rivalry, I suspect is more like it. Sounds like something that happened a long time ago. Not really our business," she added, a tinge of guilt washing over her for eavesdropping.

"Well, they did pick a public location to discuss it, whatever it is," Betty pointed out, leaning in closer. "You can't hold a conversation in a hotel lobby and expect no one to hear."

"You have to admit it was a clever idea," Lydia said.

"At the time," Helen interjected.

"It was a terrible idea. If I hadn't been feverish, I would have called it off," Deirdre said.

"Come on," Lydia persisted. "We were all tempted. We hadn't pulled anything off like that since we were kids."

"True…" Helen mused. "And we're still hearing about it after all these decades…"

Mist and Betty looked at each other and mouthed the word "decades," before leaning forward again.

"Anyone have popcorn?"

Both Mist and Betty jumped at the sound of Clive's voice. Looking over their shoulders, they saw he had come up behind them without making a sound.

"Hush," Betty whispered.

"It was just a date," Lydia said. "A trick to play on someone."

"Just a date?" Deirdre's voice rose.

"Here we go..." Helen murmured.

"You *married* him!" Deirdre exclaimed.

"Yikes!" Clive raised his hands and backed away. "This has 'catfight' written all over it. I think I'll just grab a dinner plate and take cover in the kitchen before the fur flies." His retreat was unnecessary, as the front door swung open with the arrival of the first dinner customers.

"Excuse me, ladies, I'm just gonna step around you and find some of Mist's good grub." William Guthrie's entrance broke up the heated discussion. Though he always skipped breakfast at the hotel in order to run his greasy spoon, Wild Bill's, down the road, he rarely missed dinner.

"I'll be in my room," Deirdre said, exiting the foyer.

"Suit yourself." Lydia huffed. "I'm ready for a hot meal."

"Every year..." Helen sighed as she followed Lydia into the dining area.

Mist checked over the buffet one more time before heading to the kitchen. As was her habit, the meal that night was simple, both in terms of preparation and cleanup. The following evening would be another story altogether. Half of Timberton was expected to show up for Christmas Eve dinner, as well as the hotel guests. Time always seemed to fast-forward at this point. After tonight's meal, Mist would help Betty clean up, then retire to her room to paint. She'd make it an early night, anticipating a busy morning. Between Betty's cookie exchange in the early afternoon and the upscale dinner that evening, her hands would be full. Not to mention the next day, with Christmas-morning celebrations. It was her habit to give a small gift to each guest, as well as to set out a buffet luncheon. Christmas Day always boasted festive yet casual gatherings at the hotel.

At the sound of Michael and Clara's voices, Mist stepped back into the dining room to greet them, filling their water glasses and offering wine from the beverage table.

"A lovely buffet, as always," Clara said. "I don't know how you do it, Mist. Everything is always so perfect."

Michael followed Clara's declaration with a smile and a subtle wink, which caused Mist to be grateful the soft restaurant lighting hid the blush she felt creep up her neck. "You're both so kind," she said. "But I think perfection is in the eye of the beholder."

"Isn't that beauty?" Lydia said, leaning in from the next table. "Beauty is in the eye of the beholder." Helen, seated across from her, nodded.

"It's both, isn't it?" Michael raised a glass of merlot, taking a sip after speaking. His eyes locked with Mist's, and just as she had the year before, she felt an inexplicable connection, something beyond words.

"Yes, I believe Michael is right, it is both," Mist said as she refilled water glasses at both tables. "There is beauty in everything, just as there is perfection. We have only to see it."

"Well, not everything is beautiful or perfect," William Guthrie said, jumping into the discussion. "For example, a pipe broke in my kitchen this morning, and I had to whip up a batch of coffee from that bottled stuff. You know, spring water or something like that."

"Might help your breakfast business some, Bill," a local resident called out, bringing a round of laughter.

"You heard her: perfection *in* everything," another local said. "That's not the same thing as everything being perfect."

"Yeah, I know, I know," Bill said. "Not everything's perfect." He took a bite of the sweet corn pudding and closed his eyes. "Then again some things are!"

Mist smiled and turned to Lydia and Helen. "Will your sister be joining you tonight?" she asked casually.

"Deirdre will probably be down later," Lydia said, earning a resigned glance from Helen. "She's a little moody today."

"I see," Mist said. "Well, we'll have plenty left over, if she gets hungry later." She finished filling water glasses and slipped back into the kitchen, where she joined Betty, who had already started the process of cleaning up. Working together, the dishes were done and the remaining food put away—leaving aside a plate for Deirdre, who had yet to resurface—within a mere fifteen minutes after the last guest had finished.

"Did Cathy ever come down to dinner? And Simon?" Betty asked, sitting down at the center table as Mist prepared to retire for an evening of quiet time and painting.

"Not tonight," Mist said. "I sent dinner up to their rooms. But I have a feeling they'll join us for Christmas Eve. I have some ideas to run by Cathy in the morning regarding the paintings we discussed, so we'll have a chance to talk."

"The Callahans went to Clayton's, of course," Betty said. "But they'll be here tomorrow. How are Maisie's nerves holding up?"

Mist couldn't help but smile. "She's fine now. It was just a shock finding out the woman who charged through her flower shop was Clayton's mother. She didn't expect her to arrive until the following day."

Betty laughed. "I think Mrs. Callahan was just as surprised. Maybe it was Maisie's green hair that did her in."

"Could be," Mist said, pausing briefly in the doorway on her way out. "We'll see how she reacts when it's violet."

She didn't need to see Betty's expression to know what it was.

TEN

A landscape of color stretched before Mist: crimson, chestnut, sage, mauve, taupe, indigo and more. This was her element, a realm of comfort and creative spirit. The world seemed endless with brushes, tubes, and canvas before her. In addition, her texture box sat nearby, an old cigar box she'd once found at a garage sale. Over the years, she'd filled the box with anything that might provide inspiration: a tiny feather, a scrap of sandpaper, a bottle cap with ridged edges, a smooth piece of glass from a Northern California beach.

These were the magic hours, after hungry stomachs had been traded for weary bodies, seeking slumber. In these late night moments, it didn't matter how many guests were staying overnight at the hotel. Once Mist retired to her room, she stepped into a different world, one that consumed her.

Now she looked over the art supplies and noticed the different thicknesses of the brushes and tints in the paints. From these, she would begin to design Cathy's "everything." Images had already come to her since meeting at the gallery—*clouds in the sky as she walked back to the hotel, a sprig of rosemary as she'd prepared dinner, steam rising from a ceramic mug as she'd refilled a guest's coffee.*

What did "everything" mean? From a creative viewpoint? Infinity. From a celebrity's viewpoint? Endless freedom. Gathering brushes into her hands, Mist closed her eyes and let the bristles take flight in her imagination. Like feathers, they floated with the wind, across land, across seas, skimming the top of the Eiffel Tower, tickling the cheek of a young child playing ball in Sicily, brushing an elephant's tusk in Kenya, circling a palm tree with tagua nuts in Ecuador, and drifting over cardamom in a Mumbai spice market, until they gathered above the earth in a whirlwind and returned to Mist's lap.

Yes, Mist thought. There would be endless possibilities for the arrangement of paintings Cathy desired for her wall. Or was that for *their* wall? The casual question posed by Cathy at Clive's gallery had hinted at something more.

A more pressing project called to her this evening though, and the quiet hotel provided the perfect ambiance. She clamped a miniature canvas on the side of her easel and began the first of a dozen small gifts to give out to guests on Christmas morning.

* * *

Freshly-ground French roast brewing, Mist raised both arms above her head and stretched. Anticipation of the events of the day had made it easy to rise early, in spite of painting well into the night. She'd planned a simple breakfast, just something to tide people over until the feast that evening: an egg-cheese-and-mushroom casserole, served with cantaloupe slices and croissants. A quick cleanup would allow the room to be readied easily for Betty's cookie exchange.

"Coffee ready yet?" Clive leaned in the doorway of the kitchen.

Mist smiled. It was a well-known fact that Clive popped in early to fill his coffee mug before returning to the gallery. Indeed, the hotel felt like home to him, especially now that his relationship with Betty was growing daily. Mist wondered at times if wedding bells might even be in the future for the senior couple. What a delight it would be to decorate and cook for that event. And it would definitely shorten Clive's stroll for his morning beverage.

"Mist?" Clive cleared his throat. "Coffee?"

"Oh, yes, it's almost ready." Mist said, realizing she hadn't answered. "I was just daydreaming about… the future."

"Well, if the future includes coffee, then I'm all for it."

"Yes, I imagine it does." Mist laughed.

"I'll make you a deal, Clive," Betty said, entering the kitchen in a floral bathrobe that signified early morning yet was nice enough for a potential run-in with guests. "If you fill the thermal carafes and put them out in the front entryway, we'll let you have the first cup."

"Sounds fair to me," Clive said. "I'm happy to oblige, ma'am."

Mist caught the smile on Betty's face at Clive's teasing use of the word "ma'am." His ability to make any formal statement sound country casual was one of his charms.

"Breakfast ready to go?" Betty asked, looking around the kitchen.

"All set up. Everything's out already except the casserole, which I'll pull out when the first guests arrive. We won't have many today."

"I'm sure you're right," Betty said. "Not with tonight's big feast. People will be saving their appetites for that."

"Or for your cookie exchange," Clive said, returning with a mug of coffee. "That's what's for lunch, right?"

"Only if you bring something to share, you know," Betty teased.

"You're not fooling anyone, Betty." Mist laughed. "You know Clive will be swiping cookies later from our hotel stash."

"Ah, Mist, I can't pull anything over on you, can I? Or you, Betty," Clive said with mock dismay. "And... I think I hear the first guests on the staircase. *And* the front door." He backed away from the kitchen door, knowing Mist would be heading through it with the hot casserole dish any minute.

"That'll be Clayton coming in to meet his parents for breakfast," Betty said.

"Ah, Clayton at the front door and the parents on the staircase, I guess," Clive said.

As expected, Mist pulled the casserole from the oven with two quilted mitts and whisked it out to the dining room. A knock on the back door of the kitchen accompanied her return.

"That will be Maisie," Mist said, taking off the mitts and setting them down on the table.

"You asked her to come help this morning?" Betty raised her eyebrows. "She hasn't been by the past couple of days."

"I suggested it might be nice to have help since we need to also prepare for the cookie gathering." Mist tried to hold back a grin, knowing Betty would see right through her plan.

"Does she know Clayton and his parents will be here this morning?"

Mist laughed. "I'm not about to ambush the poor girl. She knows the Callahans are meeting here." Mist turned her comment toward Maisie as she stepped into the kitchen and closed the door. "Don't you?"

"Of course I do," Maisie quipped. "You don't really need help, do you?" Her expression gave away the fact she already knew the answer.

"Hmm... no... it suddenly seems everything's under control," Mist said, looking around innocently. "Maybe you'd like to serve some coffee and then join Clayton and his parents for breakfast?"

"Exactly what I planned from the moment you tried to trick me into coming by." Maisie shed her winter coat, red woolen mittens and matching hat and set them on a stool at the center table. "Besides, I had dinner with them last night. Clayton fixed the meal... nothing like what you fix here," she added, lowering her voice. "But we all got along fine. Mrs. Callahan even said she thought my green hair was unique, not to mention appropriate for the season."

"How fun," Betty said. "You may just have to dye it red for Valentine's Day and orange for Halloween."

"Now you're talking." Maisie laughed as she left the kitchen for the dining area.

* * *

Millie, the town librarian, was the first to arrive for the cookie exchange, walking in a full ten minutes early with a tray of chocolate-chip-cherry-oatmeal cookies, still warm from the oven. "A new recipe from my cousin Sue—delicious, I might add!" She spouted off a list of ingredients.

"Good heavens, Millie," Betty said. "Is there anything that's not in those?"

"Walnuts, but you could add them." Millie laughed. "Or pecans. And Sue sometimes substitutes cinnamon for orange zest. It's fine to be creative, especially when it comes to holiday baking."

"I'm glad to hear that," Marge said, following right behind Millie. "You told us we could bend the rules this year, so I made divinity puffs. And they are divine, indeed!"

Betty took the platter of candy from Marge and set it on the buffet next to Millie's tray. "Grab some coffee or tea, ladies. We may have to test the goods while waiting for others to arrive."

Clive's voice echoed from the front hallway. "Hey, I thought I was the official tester."

"No sir," Marge said before Betty even had a chance to say the exact same thing. "If you're nice, maybe we'll share a few afterward."

"I'm kidding you all. Just came in for coffee, but I'm going back to the gallery for last-minute customers." The door closed as Clive exited but soon reopened as townsfolk began arriving with plates of delicious holiday treats. Maisie showed up with her snickerdoodles, Sally brought chocolate-chunk cookies, and Mrs. Callahan surprised everyone with candy cane brownies that she'd baked over at Clayton's house.

"I didn't know you were bringing anything," Betty exclaimed as she pointed the way to the buffet table, which was rapidly filling with tempting options.

"Clayton said it's the highlight event of Timberton's holiday season. I didn't want to miss out. Though I admit he may have had an ulterior motive for telling me that. I noticed several empty spaces on the cooling racks!"

"Yes." Sally laughed, adding a basket of cranberry-orange cookies to the array. "That seems to happen whenever my son comes to visit too."

Mist entered the room, checked the coffee and tea supply, and approached Betty. "Did Clara come downstairs yet? I know she wanted to put out those snowball cookies she made."

"I haven't seen her," Betty said, looking toward the front entry. "Oh, wait, here she comes now."

Clara entered the room wearing a light blue sweater with a snowflake pattern, and a smile on her face.

Mist felt her heart warm at the sight of a cheerful Ms. Winslow. She ushered her into the kitchen and handed her a silver tray, her cookies arranged neatly on white doilies.

"How beautiful, Mist!" Clara exclaimed. "I have some lovely family trays at home, but I don't seem to have any in my suitcase."

"This is your Christmas home, Clara," Mist said.

"I know, dear," Clara said. "You and Betty do make it feel like home. I look forward to this trip all year."

As Clara took her tray out to join the others, chatter and laughter echoed back as the kitchen door opened and closed. Mist fixed a cup of peppermint tea and sat down, enjoying the sounds of sharing and friendship floating in from the gathering. Christmas Eve was a magical day at the Timberton Hotel. And with the evening still ahead, there was more holiday cheer to come.

With apple-walnut stuffing and a large green salad ready in the refrigerator, and zucchini spice bread in the oven, Mist set a timer and retreated to her room. Later she would prepare the pork roast and ready the snap peas and sweet potatoes, but she still had work to do to prepare for Christmas morning. Attaching one miniature canvas at a time to her easel, she sat quietly, contemplating each guest staying with them this year. Each Christmas was different for the hotel, just as it was for each person. Life was ever changing. Michael Blanton, Clara Winslow, Cathy and Simon, the three sisters, Lydia, Helen and Deirdre, and the Callahans had all seen change during the past year, even during their stay in Timberton. As she pondered each guest's journey, she let her brushes and paints respond. By the time the zucchini spice bread finished baking, two miniature paintings were finished. When the roast came out of the oven later, the rest would be done.

ELEVEN

Mist lit the candles on each table in the dining room, turning Moonglow into an otherworldly vision of holiday festivity. Each flame cast light on the enchanting textures and colors of the arranged roses, hydrangea, lilies, mums and cymbidiums, as well as the copper, gold, and silver metal accents. She nudged one centerpiece lightly, hearing the intended result: the soft tinkling of silver bells. White linen tablecloths covered the oak tables, and each place setting featured a bright red linen napkin with fresh holly napkin holders, as well as a petite wooden cup, hand-painted with a pinecone design and filled with mints.

Standing alone in the room, Mist could hear the cheerful voices in the front parlor as guests and townsfolk gathered. Instrumental versions of "The Little Drummer Boy" and "O Tannenbaum" serenaded those who awaited the feast as they sipped wine or sparkling water with strawberries and lime.

"Everything's ready," Maisie whispered.

Turning toward the kitchen door, Mist took in Maisie's ivory dress and headband of holly and red berries, a distinctly softer look than the T-shirts and flower-shop overalls Maisie usually wore. *Ah, the ways of the heart*, Mist thought, knowing Clayton and his parents would be arriving soon.

"What?" Maisie said, suppressing a giggle.

"You look beautiful," Mist said.

"I'm not the only one who dressed up for Christmas Eve," Maisie pointed out.

Mist smiled. She'd had fun sprucing up the flowing green silk dress that Sally had set aside for her when it came into the thrift shop. Mist had cut and sewn the hemline into scalloped edges before attaching iridescent beads at random intervals, with additional beads scattered around the neckline and sleeves. With the extra fabric from the hem, she'd fashioned a narrow scarf that now flowed through her hair like a ribbon in the wind, sweeping most of her hair up while still allowing a single tendril to trail along the curve of her neck.

"Then I say let's open the doors," Mist said. "People await food for the stomach, heart, and soul. I believe we have all of it here within this room." She crossed to the front entryway, pausing only to flick a switch that illuminated hundreds of sparkling white lights across the ceiling before opening the doors. "Christmas Eve dinner is served," she said, the simple statement bringing cheers from the hungry crowd.

Christopher and Michelle Callahan were among the first to enter, choosing a large table that allowed Clayton and several others to join them. Two of the members of Clayton's fire crew found their way to two of the chairs, with William "Wild Bill" Guthrie and Ernie from Pops Parlor taking up two other chairs.

One chair was saved for Maisie, who alternately sat down to enjoy the meal and excused herself to help refill the buffet as the meal went on.

Lydia, Helen, and Deirdre arrived together, dressed in different outfits, yet all wearing old-fashioned pins, identical except for a stone: one red, one blue, and one green. "A gift long ago, from our grandmother," Helen said. "We wear them every Christmas."

Mist suggested a table near the buffet, pleased to see the sisters together. Though disappointments from the past didn't always go away, they could be set aside on occasion. Over time, those occasions would hopefully multiply for the Anders sisters.

As Mist carried baskets of fresh zucchini spice bread from table to table, Michael Blanton and Clara Winslow walked in, Cathy and Simon just behind them. Though a slight hush passed over the room at the sight of Cathy, it quickly settled back into casual conversation, thanks to some slight prepping by Betty, who'd explained to locals that a gift of an everyday holiday would be the best present they could offer the celebrity. The four sat together, Clara remarking that the centerpiece looked like a fantasy explosion of cheer and goodwill.

One by one, the tables filled with hotel guests and townsfolk alike. Some chose to fill plates at the buffet and take them to the front parlor, where they could sit by the fire or at one of several tables that had been set up for the expected overflow crowd.

"I say cinnamon," Millie whispered to Marge as they attempted to analyze the apple-walnut stuffing inside the roast.

"Hmm. I say nutmeg," Marge countered after taking another bite. Sally, sitting with the other two, nodded in agreement and added cloves to the growing list.

"You're all correct," Mist said, lowering her voice as she passed by the table. "And celery. Always remember celery."

"In stuffing?" The three women paused, their forks hovering in the air while waiting for Mist's answer.

"In almost everything," Mist whispered. "But don't tell William Guthrie. He's bound to add it to that coffee he serves."

"I heard that." Bill Guthrie laughed from a nearby table. "You folks ever plan to stop giving me a bad time about my coffee?"

"Not likely," Clayton said, eliciting laughs from other locals.

After offering bread to several other tables, Mist felt a light touch on one arm. She turned to see Michael indicate a chair beside him. Clara, Cathy, and Simon were engrossed in a discussion on the other side of the table. Betty conveniently swept by at the same moment, borrowing the basket of bread to continue the rounds.

"Sit and enjoy, Mist," Michael said, standing to gently guide Mist into the empty seat. "I'll make up a plate for you."

Mist accepted the seat, cautioning Michael to stick to small portions. "I had to test everything earlier, you know." She laughed.

Michael pushed her chair in and then leaned down. "You look beautiful," he whispered.

"Thank you," Mist said, the compliment both unexpected and enchanting. She took a sip of wine, obviously poured ahead with the intention of encouraging her to sit down and enjoy the meal with everyone else. Michael soon returned and sat back down. Mist thanked him again as he placed her dinner on the table in front of her.

"You're from New Orleans, I believe," Mist said, recalling past comments from Betty, as well as the contact information in the registration files.

"Yes," Michael said. "Just north of there now, actually, but my P.O. Box is New Orleans. I teach literature at LSU."

"Ah, I didn't know that, but it makes sense."

"Why is that?"

"It explains your love of reading and your knowledge of books."

Michael nodded, pensive while taking a bite of sweet potato. "I've loved to read since I was very young. I went into teaching because of that, hoping to inspire others to read."

"A noble pursuit." Mist acknowledged. "I also learned to read at an early age. It's a way to travel without traveling, to meet people without meeting them."

"Exactly," Michael said. "You understand that, but many people have yet to discover the joys of reading. We have a local literacy program that I'm involved in too."

"That must be so rewarding," Mist said. "Not only to be able to delve into the concepts and themes of books with your students but to open up whole worlds of possibility to others." She reached for a pitcher of water and proceeded to refill Michael's glass, then her own and those of others at the table.

"You're supposed to be relaxing right now, not working," Michael chided, though smiling. "You do so much to care for others here. You need to let others care for you too."

"But they do, every day. When someone laughs, it nourishes my soul. When someone's hunger is relieved, my mind rests."

"Then I can see why you're so calm all the time," Michael said. "There's no hunger in this town with your wonderful café here, so your mind must always be at rest. I also know through Betty that you feed the town's one homeless resident."

"You're talking about Hollister," Mist said. "He has a room here unofficially, an extra hotel room we don't use. He can come and go as he wishes. Easily, since that room has a back door. It also happens to have a refrigerator, and he knows he's welcome to help himself."

Michael smiled. "How nice that you just *happen* to have a refrigerator in that room."

"We need a second refrigerator to store extra supplies," Mist said simply. "That room is a convenient place to keep it."

"Of course."

Feeling a tap on her shoulder, Mist turned to see Betty leaning down. "Some guests are almost ready for dessert." Mist started to stand, but Betty shook her head. "No, Clive knows what to do; your instructions were very clear. And we have additional help too. You just keep enjoying your meal and visit with Michael here. Maisie's clearing some plates now. We'll bring the desserts out individually as people finish their meals."

"If you insist," Mist said. "Dare I ask who you have for extra help in there?"

"Someone who has plenty of practice burning food," Betty whispered.

Mist set her fork down. "You're letting William Guthrie loose in the kitchen with a blowtorch?"

"It's fine." Clayton chuckled as he looked at the other members of his fire crew. "We're here, right, boys?" Pausing, he added, "You *are* kidding, aren't you, Betty?"

"Don't worry, Clive is there to supervise. And we have a bucket of water nearby, just in case." Betty laughed.

"All right." Mist sighed, hoping not to regret the wave of trust that washed over her. "But don't forget the fresh mint—one sprig on each and the berries."

"Sounds intriguing," Michael said to Mist as Betty turned away. "What should I expect to see coming from the kitchen, aside from flames?"

"Something simple this year."

"Which would not be a fire..." Clayton noted.

"Probably *not* simple, coming from you. But simply delicious, I imagine," Michael said.

"I hope so."

Minutes later, Betty emerged from the kitchen with a dessert in each hand, Maisie right behind her with two more. Mist smiled with approval as they passed by, her fear of disaster replaced by the sight of perfectly caramelized sugar.

"Crème brûlée?" Cathy said from across the table. "I recognize the fluted ramekins."

Mist nodded. "Excellent guess. I decided an orange-vanilla bean crème brûlée would be a light finishing touch to the meal this year."

"With a sprig of mint," Michael added.

"Yes, and candied cranberries," Mist said, "for a touch of holiday color."

"Speaking of color, I love all the decorations, Mist," Clara said. "The table centerpieces, the Christmas tree, the poinsettias along the staircase—everything is so welcoming and comforting."

"I agree completely," Cathy said. "Warm and cozy, in the most wonderful way. I haven't had a Christmas this enjoyable in ages. I feel more at home here than I do... well, at home."

"We especially love the wreath of bells on the front door." Deirdre added, leaning over from another table. Both Lydia and Helen nodded in agreement.

Betty and Maisie made repeat trips to and from the kitchen, empty plates heading one direction, individual crème brûlée servings returning to take their places. One by one, guests finished dessert and retired to the front parlor, drawn by strains of Bing Crosby's "Do You Hear What I Hear?"

Sparkling lights from the hotel's Christmas tree formed a glowing background to old-fashioned ornaments: a pair of hand-knit red mittens, a clip-on glass bird with feathers, a blue-rimmed tin drum, and a miniature wooden nutcracker. Along with those, Clive's new addition nestled in the rear of the tree, undetected. As Betty brought fresh coffee out from the kitchen, Clive steered her toward the tree and lifted a silver ornament from between the branches. Betty gasped in delight at the sight of two silver bells dangling from a red ribbon.

"Needle and thread, anyone?" Mist indicated a basket of supplies and two bowls.

"Popcorn and cranberry garlands!" Lydia exclaimed. "We always made those when we were growing up. Remember?" She directed her question at both sisters, whose eyes lit up at the childhood memory.

"I'll join in," Clara said, taking a chair nearby.

"You could always make one to take home with you, Clara. You know, with that plate of cookies from the exchange," Mist suggested, earning a shy smile in return. A second smile came from Michael, who'd settled into his usual chair by the fireplace. In fact, not a face in the crowd was without a glow as Mist surveyed the relaxed, festive group.

"What an exquisite piano," Simon said, noticing an upright piano in the corner, halfway between the Christmas tree and fireplace.

"It was my father's," Betty said. "I don't play, but I keep it tuned for guests. The piano tuner who comes down from Helena always seems impressed with it."

"As well he should be," Simon said. "Most people are familiar with Steinway and Sons, but these Knabes are fine instruments, with a unique tonal quality that is hard to match." His eyes traveled to Cathy, who had joined the garland activity. He raised his eyebrows and then nodded, turning back to Betty. "May I?" He indicated the piano bench.

"Of course," Betty said quickly.

"One moment." Mist crossed the room and opened a small closet, turning the recorded music off. When she turned back, Simon was seated at the piano, Cathy standing beside him. A hush fell across the room as Simon ran deft fingers over the keys, periodically resting on a chord.

"I can't tell you how happy I am to not have fifty thousand people in this room tonight," Cathy said, earning a laugh all around. She paused as Simon worked up a short intro to "O Holy Night" and then began to sing, her voice strong and emotional, crystal clear and sweeter than sugar on crème brûlée. By the time she'd finished, there wasn't a dry eye in the room. Begged for an encore, she insisted she'd only sing if others joined in. At first hesitant, the holiday spirit came alive as hotel guests and townsfolk alike joined in as Simon led everyone through a musical set of sing-along Christmas classics ranging from "Frosty the Snowman" to "Santa Claus is Coming to Town." When he wrapped up the set with "The Twelve Days of Christmas," he sped the tempo up as the song progressed until not only were the participants unable to keep up with which day it was, but they could barely sing for laughing so hard.

The evening continued in the same spirit. Others took turns at the piano. No one matched Simon's expertise, but each had just as great a time playing. Clayton and Maisie bundled up and went for a walk, snow flurries setting a romantic backdrop. Mist settled beside the fire with Michael, engrossed in a discussion of symbolism and imagery in American literature. Cathy struck a deal with one of the fire crew to sign an autograph for him only if he signed one for her. This triggered a hysterical exchange between others, with Timberton's own next-door neighbors signing autographs for each other before even realizing that's what they were doing. Many would later blame that on eggnog and rum.

Eventually the gathering quieted down, with townsfolk taking their leave and guests retiring to their rooms, until only Betty and Mist remained.

"A lovely Christmas Eve, Mist," Betty said. "Very cheerful."

"I do believe you're right." Mist surveyed the empty room, pleased. "With more cheer to come tomorrow."

TWELVE

Not yet dawn, Mist slipped down the hallway and turned on the Christmas tree lights. She moved to the fireplace and struck a match, grateful Clive had prepared a fire the night before, long after the evening's camaraderie had ended. Tiptoeing to the kitchen, she set the coffee to brew, slipped a tray of currant scones in the oven, and returned to watch the fire grow. Barefoot, hair loose, she sat in front of the tree, her eggshell-white rayon gown softly folding on the floor around her. In the silent room, with only the sparkling lights and glow of the fire for company, she thought over the past few days. This year's guests had presented no unusual challenges or drama, yet each had an ongoing story. It was as if a film had paused midway through, or a resting place had appeared along a path. Was this what the visit felt like to each guest? She hoped so.

Reaching forward, she adjusted the angle of one of many packages she'd placed under the tree shortly after midnight. It had taken only an hour or so after the hotel had settled for the night to finish the miniature paintings she'd started soon after the guests first arrived. Now each gift waited, wrapped in fabric swatches and raffia, to be claimed.

She closed her eyes and let herself be lulled by the warmth of the fire. A soft wind whistled outside. There would be new snowfall when the sun began its Christmas Day ascent into the Montana sky. Flurries had already started by the time townsfolk headed home the night before.

Sensing a presence behind her, Mist opened her eyes but didn't turn her head. She didn't need to in order to know who was there.

"Like an angel." The soft words almost blended in with the wind.

"An angel, you say? Like the one at the top of the tree?" Mist looked up. "I've always loved that one, with her faded voile wings and slender candle in her hands."

"No," Michael said. "Like the one in front of the tree."

Mist wondered momentarily if it was possible to blush in the dark. Or if, instead, it was like the proverbial tree falling in the forest; was there sound if no one could hear? Was there color if no one could see?

The sound of the front door opening saved Mist from contemplating sound and sight. She stood up, turned, and met Michael's eyes. "That will be Clive, sneaking in for the first cup of coffee. Would you like a cup too?"

"Coffee sounds wonderful," Michael said. He stepped aside as Clive entered, stomping his feet on the way in to shake off a layer of snow.

"I'm not the first one in line for coffee this morning, I see," Clive said. He glanced around the room, took in the sparkling Christmas tree, cozy fire, and first rays of light filtering in through the front window, and nodded with approval.

"Nor the last," Betty chimed in from the kitchen. "We have a full pot coming right up." She appeared a minute later, a large thermal carafe in each hand and a Santa hat on her head with "Betty" embroidered across the white fur brim. She set the carafes down and executed a dramatic curtsey to show off her Christmas-morning outfit.

"Well, aren't you just the picture of a perfect Mrs. Claus," Clive said, clearly delighted.

"I'm so glad you said so," Betty chirped, pulling out a matching hat from behind the registration counter. She placed it on Clive's head, adjusting it to best display his own embroidered name.

Mist took advantage of Betty and Clive's banter to set soft Christmas music and then slip back to her room. Other guests would soon hear the early morning sounds of the hotel stirring and join in to fill their own coffee cups and exchange Christmas greetings. She reemerged in a soft red sweater, patchwork skirt, and trademark work boots, her hair swept back and clipped up above her neck. A sprig of holly peeked out of a silver barrette. Passing through the kitchen, she pulled the double trays of scones from the oven, let them cool a few minutes, and returned to the front parlor, setting the warm baked goods beside the coffee service, as well as a bowl of fresh-cut melon and berries. The simple morning fare would leave room for a heartier brunch later on.

Michael refilled his coffee as Mist tended the casual breakfast buffet. "*Bach's Christmas Oratorio*," he said.

"Yes." Mist smiled, not at all surprised to find he recognized the traditional classical piece. "Just the first two parts, with Handel's *Messiah* to follow next."

"Perhaps Liszt's *Christmas Tree Suite* after that?"

Mist shook her head. "An excellent suggestion, but I believe Bach and Handel are opening acts for Frank Sinatra, Andy Williams, and Johnny Mathis."

"Ah, Johnny Mathis," Michael said. "'Silver Bells.'"

"Right again." Mist smiled as she turned to greet Clara, who descended the staircase in a green velour pantsuit with a festive vest of sequined reindeer and candy canes.

"Let me guess," Clara said. "You made that skirt in keeping with your creative spirit."

"She's guilty as charged," Sally said, arriving with Marge and Millie right behind her. "She collects bits and pieces of fabric whenever I get them in." The three women all took scones and either coffee or tea and settled down at a table toward the back of the front parlor. Though they knew townsfolk were always welcome at the hotel, they respected the overnight guests and wanted to allow them prime seating near the fireplace.

A few at a time, guests emerged from their rooms, helped themselves to hot beverages, fruit and baked goods, and settled in the front parlor. Cathy's entrance attracted notice, not so much for her well-known status, but for the simple elegance of her ivory turtleneck, emerald earrings, and casual ponytail of curls pulled back with a red silk ribbon. Even paired with basic jeans and simple flats, the look was stunning on her.

By the time the Callahans and Clayton joined in, the hotel guests had gathered around the tree. Frank Sinatra's voice in the background offered wishes for all to have "a merry little Christmas." Mist reached under the tree and pulled out the first item. "I have something for each of you, as a thank-you for spending your holiday here at the Timberton Hotel. You enrich our lives here in this small town with your visits." She looked around the room, her gaze resting first on Clara. Reaching out, she handed her the fabric-covered gift, which Clara opened.

"How clever and sweet!" Clara exclaimed, holding the miniature painting up for all to see. "Now that's a trail I'd definitely follow," she said, pointing to a rustic sign with a simple arrow and a plate of assorted cookies. The path beyond it was light, with a few unexpected turns. Mist was actually delighted that Clara failed to notice one of the cookies was heart-shaped. She had a feeling Clara would discover it later, when she looked more closely.

"Now those," Maisie whispered, pointing at a pair of gifts on a low branch.

"Yes, good idea." Mist agreed, taking the presents and handing them to the Callahans. "I felt unsure of what to paint for the two of you since you've been here to visit with Clayton and we haven't seen as much of you as other guests. Fortunately Maisie came to my rescue with some inspiration. One of these is for you,

Clayton, the other for your parents." Clayton and his mother opened the gifts and held the paintings up for others to see.

"Flowers," Lydia said, "and gorgeous ones at that."

"Absolutely beautiful," Michelle Callahan agreed. "And unless I'm imagining it, all the flowers in these paintings are varieties I picked up in your store, Maisie."

"Very true," Maisie said. "You loved them so much. I always wish flowers would last longer, especially for those who appreciate them. This way you can have them year-round."

"So thoughtful," Michelle said, giving Maisie a hug. "And beautiful artwork, Mist. Thank you."

Mist reached under the tree and lifted up three packages, identical at first glance, but tied with raffia in different colors. She handed one to each of the three sisters, who opened them and held them up.

"The silver bell wreath from the front door," Lydia said, delighted. "I adore that wreath."

"Yes," Helen agreed. "It's so welcoming. And the soft echo of bells each time the door opens and closes is enchanting."

Deirdre nodded in agreement. "And look, mine has a blue ribbon, how delightful." Lydia and Helen checked their wreath paintings, noting the red and green ribbons on each.

"Very clever, Mist," Betty said, watching from the side of the room. "Identical wreaths with individually colored ribbons. Like those lovely pins you all wore at dinner last night."

"That's partially true, but not entirely," Mist said. She picked up three magnifying glasses from the fireplace mantel and handed one to each sister. "Look at the wreaths in detail."

Lydia, Helen, and Deirdre inspected the paintings more closely with the magnifying glasses, trading them back and forth.

"They look the same," Deirdre began, "but... wait, that's not entirely true. Helen, does yours have a green tint to one of the silver bells at the bottom?"

Helen shook her head. "No, definitely nothing green. Does yours have a yellow flower on a bell to the right?"

"Where do you see that?" Deirdre asked.

Helen pointed to her painting and then looked at Deirdre's. "No, you don't."

"I don't have one either," Lydia said. "But there's a sliver of gold running through mine, just a trace, like the ribbons that run through the centerpieces in the dining room."

Each sister alternated discoveries.

"A tiny candy cane!"

"Light blue stripes."

"A crescent moon."

"They're not at all the same when we look closely," Lydia said. "How very clever." She paused, thinking. "I still want the one with the red bow though."

All three sisters traded again, ending with the color they'd originally opened.

Mist reached into the tree again, first pulling out a single package, then putting it back. She pulled two others out, instead, and handed them to Cathy and Simon.

"Open yours first," Cathy said, nudging Simon's arm. He removed the raffia and fabric, looked at the painting, and grinned.

"Thank you, Mist. When on earth did you paint this? You must have done this late last night," Simon added, answering his own question. He turned the painting toward the rest of the group, exhibiting a striking image of the piano he had just played the night before. "It's wonderful, the painting, the piano itself... oh, that tone!" He turned to Cathy. "Your turn."

Mist could sense the expectant current running through the room. What would one give someone who had everything? Who could purchase anything? The sense of anticipation grew even stronger when Cathy opened the package and simply smiled, even wiped a tear from her eye. The anticipation turned to confusion when she turned the canvas around.

"It's blank," Clive said, scratching his chin.

"Yes, it is," Cathy said, her smile stretching from one dazzling earring to the other.

"How wonderful," Michael said, meeting Mist's eyes.

"I must be missing something," Clayton said, precipitating a few similar murmurs.

"No, you're not," Mist said. "But Cathy is, and I believe it's this." She reached above the fireplace mantel again, this time lifting a slender paintbrush, which she handed to Cathy. A red ribbon trailed beyond the length of the brush, giving it the illusion of a magic wand.

"I used to paint," Cathy explained to the mystified room. "But with my schedule... I just put it aside. Mist knows I've missed it." She set the canvas in her lap, the brush on top of it. "This may be the most beautiful gift I've ever received. Thank you, Mist."

The sound of a man clearing his throat nearby caused Cathy to look at Simon and then quickly raise a hand to one ear. "Oh, yes, of course! The earrings aren't too shabby either."

The guests clapped at Cathy's quick response. While the room buzzed with the sudden inside knowledge that the relationship between Cathy and Simon was more than just celebrity and bodyguard, Mist took the last package from the tree and handed it to Michael, who untied the raffia and slid the canvas out.

"Remarkable," Michael said. "With every detail, you've captured the essence of this wonderful old hotel. It couldn't be any clearer if I stood on the sidewalk and looked at the front of the building myself."

"Where's the snow, Mist?" Clive asked, taking a look. "The paintings you send home with guests always represent something to remind them of their stay here, right?"

"Look closely, Clive." Betty pointed to the lower half of the painting. "The garden is filled with columbine, iris, and hollyhock. Look at the tulips along the front walk and the clematis on the trellis."

"You're telling me there's no snow because it's not winter," Clive said.

"Now you're catching on, Clive." Betty laughed. "Took you long enough, considering you've seen the hotel look like this from April through August for years. How about another cup of coffee? I have a fresh pot brewing."

"So this is what the Timberton Hotel looks like in the spring," Michael said after Betty led Clive away by the elbow. "It's wonderful, just as you've described it—such an explosion of color where now there's only white." He held the painting at arm's length as if imagining the view from the street. "How should I interpret this painting?"

"Interpretation is in the mind of the beholder," Mist said.

"Like beauty, like perfection."

"Exactly."

THIRTEEN

"A lovely Christmas," Betty said as she and Mist dried and put away breakfast dishes. The day after Christmas was calm compared to the previous day. Timberton residents and guests had continued to celebrate throughout the day, enjoying meals at either the hotel or their own homes. They listened to music, exchanged gifts, and even bundled up for winter walks when the snowfall paused in the afternoon and the sun appeared.

"I'm sure the guests will treasure the paintings you gave them," Betty continued. "It's wonderful that you send them home with memories of their holiday vacation. Or thoughts of the future," she added, a twinkle in her eye.

"Memories can be from the past, present, or future," Mist said.

"Of course," Betty said. She smiled at Clive, who sat at the center island, shaking his head. Though Betty was growing used to Mist's perception of the world, Clive had a ways to go.

"I saw that, you two." Mist laughed.

"Come on," Betty said. "You can't blame us for sharing a grin. We're fond of you and always intrigued with the way you view the world. Speaking of 'memories of the future,' it's clear that Michael Blanton is quite smitten with you."

"It's possible," Mist said.

"Ha!" Clive laughed. "We saw you take that long afternoon walk when the sun came out. You must have had time to talk. You can't blame us for being curious."

"OK, you're right," Mist said. "We did get a chance to talk."

"I knew it." Betty hustled over to a stool beside Clive and took a seat. "Spill it. What did you talk about?"

"Hmm… well, let's see," Mist said. "Since you're both so curious…"

"Ah, there you go." Clive circled one hand in a forward motion, encouraging Mist to continue.

"First…" Mist paused, just for the pleasure of suspense. "First we discussed one of Immanuel Kant's concepts: that forms of consciousness require prior conditions that enable possibility."

"Oh," Betty and Clive both said, their expressions blank. "Then what?"

Mist poured a mug of peppermint tea and sat down across from them, hands wrapped around the ceramic surface.

"Well, Michael recently attended a performance of Bach's *Goldberg Variations* when the New York Philharmonic performed in New Orleans. I think it's fascinating how a piece written for harpsichord can carry forward to modern piano. He thinks it's a natural progression, but I'm not so sure."

"I see," Clive said. "Maybe Simon would have an opinion about that."

"You may be onto something there, Clive," Mist said.

"Mist, you're making us crazy here," Betty said. "What else?"

Mist took a sip of tea and lowered her cup. "Sustainability issues in tourism. Machu Picchu, for example."

"I understand that one," Clive said proudly.

"You do?" Betty raised one eyebrow.

"Of course," Clive said. "It means when too many people go to the same place, it can get mighty messed up."

"Exactly," Mist said. "And 'mighty messed up' is a good way to put it, Clive."

"Is that all?" Betty said. "Nothing more interesting? Hmm?"

"Let's see… his nephew has a turtle named Aloysius."

"Would not have guessed that one," Clive murmured.

"Really," Mist continued. "There's nothing exciting to report from the walk. You two matchmakers may now return to your regularly scheduled programming."

"But he's obviously smitten," Betty said, leading the discussion right back to where it started.

"It's possible," Mist said.

* * *

"Thank you for another wonderful Christmas." Clara gave Betty and Mist each a warm embrace.

"I hope your new gentleman friend enjoys the container of cookies," Betty said. "We came up with a good variety at this year's cookie exchange."

"I'm sure he will," Clara said. "He's such a nice man. You would both like him."

"Maybe we'll get to meet him someday," Betty said.

"Who knows?" Clara laughed.

"Life is full of unexpected adventures, isn't it?" Mist gave Clara another hug. Clive, who had been standing nearby, picked up Clara's suitcase and walked her out to her rental car.

"That's just about everyone," Betty said as she waved to Clara and closed the front door. "The Callahans left this morning; Clayton and Maisie drove them to the airport. A driver picked Cathy and Simon up shortly after that. And the sisters took off about an hour ago."

"I guess that just leaves me." The sound of Michael's voice accompanied his footsteps on the stairs. He set his suitcase down. "Wonderful holiday as always, Betty."

"Thank you, Michael," Betty said. "I'm so happy you came to spend Christmas at the Timberton Hotel as always. I look forward to seeing you every year."

"The feeling is mutual," Michael said. He gave Betty a hug, watched her disappear into the kitchen, and then turned back to Mist. "How about seeing me out? Or better yet, just to the door. It's cold outside and you don't have a jacket on."

"I'd be delighted to escort you the entire twenty feet or so," Mist said, laughing as she looked across to the front door.

Michael picked up his suitcase and crossed the foyer, Mist just a few steps behind. She reached for the doorknob, hesitated briefly, and then opened it.

A gust of cold air blew in, along with light flurries of new snowfall. Michael stepped out and turned around.

"Thank you for a wonderful Christmas, Mist. Betty has always been the perfect host, but you make everything just a little more perfect."

"You are too kind, Michael. But you know, we all…"

"Yes." Michael laughed. "I already know what you're going to say. We all make the holidays special for each other. I do believe I'm beginning to see the world through your eyes."

Mist smiled but remained quiet. He was right, he did see the world the way she did. A few seconds passed in silence. Another gust of wind brought a new wave of snow flurries onto the porch. Michael glanced up, and Mist followed his gaze, which rested on a red ribbon dangling from a cluster of mistletoe pinned above the doorway.

"That wasn't there before." Mist looked at the traditional Christmas symbol, certain she'd tied it to the staircase bannister when decorating the hotel.

"I know," Michael said.

"Strange that it could move around on its own," she murmured.

"Strange, indeed." Michael set his suitcase down and rested one arm on the doorframe, sheltering Mist from the wind. "May I?" He searched her face and then slowly leaned forward and placed a light kiss on her forehead.

"I'm supposed to say yes now, I think…"

"It would be nice," Michael said, amused.

"Well, then… yes."

"That's what I was hoping to hear."

Cool snowflakes mixed with the warmth of Michael's gentle kiss, a gesture that spoke of kindness, passion, and promise in equal measure.

"Merry Christmas, Mist." He smiled, picked up his suitcase, and walked to his car. With a wave of his hand, he was off.

Mist stepped back inside the hotel and closed the door, hearing the soft echo of the wreath's bells. She raised her hand to her face, touched her lips with her fingertips, and then headed to the kitchen.

"What?" Mist tried to contain a smile when she saw Betty leaning against the sink counter, an expectant look on her face, but she couldn't.

"Well, good." Betty sighed. "That makes this easy." She looked down at two envelopes, one in each hand, and held one up. "I was told to give you this one if you didn't come back smiling." She then held up the other. "And to give you this one if you *were* smiling, which you are."

Betty motioned to the center counter. "The notes go with this, at least one does."

Mist followed Betty's arm gesture, finding a bouquet of flowers loosely arranged in a ceramic vase. "Why, they're beautiful! So many colors: yellow, peach, blue, pale pink. How on earth?"

"Maisie had to do some scrambling to pull this assortment together," Betty said.

Mist leaned over to breathe in the mixed fragrances of the blooms. "I think you'd better let me see that note. No, make that both notes."

"Both notes?" Betty stalled, debating. "Okay, here's the first one—the one I was told to give you if you *weren't* smiling when you came back in." She handed the note over to Mist, who opened the sealed envelope, puzzled.

Because you are special...

"How sweet," Mist said. "Strange that would be the note to give me if I hadn't been smiling."

"I suppose that depends on what the other one says." Betty held out the second note, which Mist immediately tore open.

"Tell me," Betty urged, seeing the smile on Mist's face spread even wider.

Mist turned back to the flowers and set the note in front of the arrangement so Betty could take a look.

See you in the spring...

"Now I understand," Betty said. "He didn't want you to feel pressured, so he set up two alternate messages."

"Even though I gave him the painting of the hotel in the spring?"

Betty shook her head. "He set this up with Maisie before you gave him the painting."

"So we each gave the other a hint about a possible visit earlier than next Christmas? Without knowing what the other was doing?"

"Apparently so," Betty said.

"That's…" Mist found herself at a loss for words.

"Sweet, Mist." Betty filled in. "That's very sweet."

Mist sat down, looked at the flowers, at the note, and reached for the reservation book, flipping back through the last few pages. "It was a nice Christmas, Betty. Look at the guests we had this year: Clara, the Callahans, Michael, Lydia, Helen and Deirdre, and Simon and Belinda Myers, who wasn't Belinda Myers at all."

"As you said yourself, Mist, anyone could be anyone, or something like that."

Mist nodded. "Yes. But you know what? Not any Christmas can be any Christmas. Each one is unique."

"That certainly seems to be true," Betty said. "I wonder what next Christmas will bring."

"We'll just have to see," Mist said, smiling. "Yes, we'll just have to see."

BETTY'S COOKIE
EXCHANGE RECIPES

Glazed Cinnamon Nuts
Cranberry Orange Cookies
Swedish Dream Cookies
Pecan Cookies
Candy Cane Brownies
Chocolate Chip Cherry Oatmeal Cookies
Thumbprint Cookies
Chocolate Chunk Cookies
Jumbles
Eggnog Cookies
Peppermint Candy Canes
Divinity Puffs
Snickerdoodles
Sharon's Chocolate Chip Cookies
Odessa's Pumpkin Cookies
Sugar Cookie Cut-Outs
Flourless Peanut Butter Chocolate Chip Cookies
Snowball Cookies
Grandma's Opera Fudge
Dutch Sour Cream Cookies
Soft Raisin Cookies
Blueberry Oatmeal Cookies

GLAZED CINNAMON NUTS
(A family recipe)

Ingredients:

1 cup sugar
1/4 cup water
1/8 teaspoon cream of tartar
Heaping teaspoon of cinnamon
1 tablespoon butter
1 1/2 cups walnut halves

Directions:

Boil sugar, water, cream of tartar and cinnamon to soft ball stage (236°F.)

Remove from heat.

Add butter and walnuts.

Stir until walnuts separate.

Place on wax paper to cool.

CRANBERRY-ORANGE COOKIES
(Submitted by Kim McMahan Davis)

Makes approximately 45 small cookies

Ingredients:

3/4 cup (4.7 ounces) dried cranberries
3/4 cup (5.3 ounces) granulated sugar
2 cups (9 ounces) all-purpose flour
1-1/2 teaspoons baking powder
1/2 teaspoon salt
1/2 cup (4 ounces) cold butter, cut into small pieces
1 egg, lightly beaten
1/4 cup orange juice
1/4 teaspoon orange extract
1/2 teaspoon red gel food coloring (optional)
Red and white coarse sugar, for rolling

Directions:

Using a food processor, pulse the dried cranberries and sugar together until the cranberries are finely ground.

Add the flour, baking powder, and salt. Pulse to combine.

Add the cold butter pieces and pulse to incorporate, until the mixture is the size of small peas. This can take about 20 pulses.

Whisk the orange juice, egg, orange extract, and food coloring (if using) in a small bowl.

Drizzle the orange juice mixture over the flour mixture in the food processor and pulse until a dough forms.

Place the dough in a bowl and cover tightly with plastic wrap. Refrigerate for at least 1 hour.

Preheat the oven to 350ºF.

Place 1/4 cup red coarse sugar and 1/4 cup white coarse sugar in a shallow bowl and mix. Set aside.

Scoop the cookie dough into 1-inch to 1-1/2-inch balls, then roll in the coarse sugar mixture. Place the sugar-coated dough on a parchment-lined baking sheet, 12 cookies to each sheet.

Bake 12 to 16 minutes or until the tops of the cookies are just set and the bottom of the cookies are barely golden. Remove from the oven and cool for 5 minutes on the baking sheet, then transfer to a wire rack to cool completely. Store in an airtight container for up to 5 days.

SWEDISH DREAM COOKIES (DRÖMKAKOR)
(Submitted by Kathy Tucker)

Called dream cookies because they are light and airy, these melt in your mouth

Makes 40-45 cookies

Ingredients:

1 2/3 cups flour
1 teaspoon baking soda
1 1/4 cups sugar
8 tablespoons, unsalted butter, softened (1 stick)
1 1/4 cups sugar
1 tablespoon vanilla sugar
1/3 cup corn oil

Directions:

Heat oven to 300°F. In a small bowl, whisk together flour and baking soda; set aside. In a large bowl and using a handheld mixer on medium speed, beat butter and sugars until pale and fluffy, 1-2 minutes. Add oil and mix until smooth. Add dry ingredients and stir until just combined.

Using a tablespoon-size measuring spoon, divide dough into about 40 portions. Using your hands, shape the dough portions into balls 2 inches apart on baking sheets lined with parchment paper.

Bake 1 sheet at a time until cookies crack on top and are just set, 25-30 minutes.

Transfer to a wire rack and let cool before serving.

PECAN COOKIES
(Submitted by Jan Harvey)

Ingredients:

2 cups butter (4 sticks)
1/2 cup sugar
4 scant cups of flour
1 1/2 cups chopped pecans

Directions:

Combine all ingredients and roll into balls the size of a walnut. Bake at 375°F for 15-20 minutes. While cookies are warm – roll in powdered sugar.

CANDY CANE BROWNIES
(Submitted by Kim McMahan Davis)

Ingredients:

Brownies

3 sticks (1-1/2 cups) butter	3/4 teaspoon peppermint
3 cups sugar	extract
5 eggs	3/4 cup cocoa powder
1 teaspoon salt	2-1/4 cups all-purpose flour

Frosting

4 tablespoons butter
2 cups confectioners' sugar
2 tablespoons heavy whipping cream
1/2 teaspoon peppermint extract

Garnish

Coarsely broken candy canes

Directions:

Brownies

Preheat oven to 350°F.

Whisk flour with the cocoa powder and set aside.
Cream butter and sugar with an electric mixer.
Beat in eggs, one at a time.
Add salt and peppermint extract and mix well.
Gradually add in the cocoa and flour mixture and stir until completed incorporated.

Line a jelly roll pan (15-1/2"x10-1/2"x1") with parchment paper. Spritz the parchment paper with non-stick cooking spray. Spread the batter evenly in the prepared pan.

Bake for about 30 minutes or until a wooden skewer inserted in the middle comes out clean. Rest pan on a wire rack until completely cool before proceeding with frosting.

Frosting

Mix the butter and confectioners' sugar together until butter is incorporated completely. Add the heavy whipping cream, 1 tablespoon at a time, whipping well after each addition. Add the peppermint extract and whip for an additional 2 minutes.

Frost the brownies then cut into 2-inch squares. Garnish each square with bits of broken candy canes right before serving.

Chocolate Chip Cherry Oatmeal Cookies
(Submitted by Sue Doucette)

Ingredients:

3/4 cup good semisweet chocolate chips
3/4 cup chopped dried sweet cherries
1 teaspoon finely grated orange zest
1 teaspoon vanilla
1/4 cup water
1 cup brown sugar
3/4 cup shortening or butter
1/2 granulated sugar
1 egg
3 cups uncooked oatmeal or quick oatmeal (don't use steel cut)
1 cup flour
1 teaspoon salt
1/2 teaspoon baking soda

Directions:

Heat oven to 350°F.

Beat brown sugar, sugar, shortening or butter. Add water, beaten egg and vanilla.
Add dry ingredients and orange zest and mix into the above mixture in small batches. Fold in chocolate chips and cherries.

Use a small ice cream scoop to scoop equal sized cookie dough balls and place on an ungreased cookie sheet.

Bake 12-15 minutes depending upon size of scoop.

Cool on a cooling rack and enjoy.

Option: substitute a little cinnamon for the orange zest.

Thumbprint Cookies
(Submitted by Jan Harvey)

Ingredients:

1/2 cup shortening
1/2 cup butter
1 egg yolk (save white)
1/2 teaspoon vanilla
1 cup sifted flour
1/4 teaspoon salt
Chopped walnuts

Directions:

Mix together shortening, butter, egg yolk and vanilla.

Sift together flour and salt. Stir into shortening mixture.

Roll into 1 inch balls. Dip in slightly beaten egg white. Roll in finely chopped walnuts.

Place 1 inch apart on ungreased cookie sheet. Bake 5 minutes at 375°F.

Remove from oven and place a candy cherry in center. Return to oven and bake 8 minutes longer. Cool.

Gluten-free Chocolate Chunk Cookies
(Submitted by Kim McMahan Davis)

These cookies use whole grain flour, to boost the nutritional value... but they're still delicious and make a satisfying dessert! Buckwheat is a gluten-free grain, despite its name. If you prefer, you can use brown rice flour instead, or if gluten is not an issue, substitute equal amounts of white whole-wheat flour.

Ingredients:

1 cup (7.5 ounces) packed brown sugar
1/3 cup canola oil
1/3 cup butter, room temperature
2 tablespoons honey
1-1/2 teaspoons vanilla extract (make sure to use a gluten-free brand if necessary, or omit)
1 large egg, room temperature
2 cups (9 ounces) Buckwheat flour (use the lightly spoon and level method if not using a scale)
1 teaspoon baking soda
1/2 teaspoon salt
4 ounces premium semisweet or bittersweet chocolate, chopped
1/2 teaspoon Fleur de sel or other coarse sea salt (optional)

Directions:

Preheat oven to 375°F.

Add brown sugar, canola oil, butter, honey, and vanilla extract to the bowl of a standing mixer. Beat on medium until well combined.

Add the egg and beat until thoroughly incorporated.

Whisk together the flour, baking soda, and salt.

Add the flour mixture to the sugar mixture and beat on low speed until blended together.

Add the chocolate and mix by hand until just incorporated.

Place rounded tablespoon-sized pieces of cookie dough on a parchment-lined baking sheet. Sprinkle a bit of the Fleur de sel over each cookie, if desired.

Bake 8 to 11 minutes until the edges start to brown. Remove the baking sheet from the oven and allow the cookies to cool on the sheet for 5 minutes, then place them on a wire rack to cool completely. Store in an airtight container in a cool, dry place.

Makes about 24 cookies, depending on size.

Jumbles
(Submitted by Linda Smith)

Ingredients:

3/4 cup pecan halves
1 1/4 cups whole almonds
1/2 cup sugar
1/4 cup brown sugar
8 tablespoons (1 stick) butter
1 egg
3/4 teaspoon vanilla

1 cup + 2 tablespoon flour
1 teaspoon baking soda
1/4 teaspoon salt
1 cup semisweet chocolate chips
1 1/2 cups raisins

Directions:

Preheat oven to 375°F.

Place the nuts on cookie sheet. Bake them, stirring occasionally, for about 7 minutes or until they begin to have a toasted aroma. Do not bake until the almond skins begin to crack. Cool completely. Chop into very coarse pieces.

Cream the sugars and butter until light and fluffy. Beat in the egg and vanilla until well blended.
Sift the flour, baking soda and salt. On low speed, beat in the flour mixture until incorporated.

In a large bowl, stir together the chocolate chips, raisins, pecans and almonds. Empty the batter into the bowl and mix together evenly with a large spoon or spatula.

Drop batter by rounded teaspoons onto the cookie sheets. Bake for 12-15 minutes or until golden brown – will still be somewhat soft inside.

EGGNOG COOKIES
(Submitted by Frances Hampton)

Ingredients:

3 1/2 cups all-purpose flour
1/2 teaspoon baking soda
1/2 teaspoon ground nutmeg
1/2 teaspoon salt
16 tablespoons unsalted butter (2 sticks) *softened on counter 1 hour*
3/4 cup granulated sugar
1/4 cup light brown sugar, packed
1 large egg
1/2 cup eggnog

Eggnog Glaze

2 cups powdered sugar *(for thicker glaze use 2 1/2 cups)*
2 tablespoons clear vanilla extract *(this makes the glaze white and not brownish white if using regular vanilla extract.)*
3 tablespoons eggnog

Directions:

In a large bowl, sift together the flour, baking soda, nutmeg, and salt.

Using a mixer, beat softened butter, granulated sugar, and brown sugar on medium-high speed until fluffy, about 2 minutes. Add egg and beat until combined. Reduce speed to low, add flour mixture, and mix until combined. Do not overmix!

Add eggnog and mix 3 times with a spatula, until combined. Do not overmix!

Divide dough into 4 pieces, wrap in plastic wrap, and refrigerate for at least 1 hour.

Preheat oven to 375°F. Line two large baking sheets with parchment paper or silicone baking mats. Set aside.

In a medium sized bowl, whisk together powdered sugar, vanilla extract, and eggnog until smooth. Set aside.
Roll out dough to about 1/8 inch thick. Using a cookie cutter, cut dough into shapes.

Place cookie shapes onto prepared baking pan. Bake for 8-10 minutes. Let cookies cool on baking sheet for 10 minutes, then transfer to wire rack. Let cookies cool completely before icing and decorating. Once cookies are cooled, dip cookies into glaze and sprinkle with colored sprinkles. Place cookies on baking sheet to set for at least 30 minutes before serving. To speed up the setting time, place cookies in the fridge for about 10-15 minutes.

Peppermint Candy Canes
(Submitted by Jan Harvey)

Ingredients:

1/2 cup shortening
1/2 cup sugar
1 egg yolk
1 1/2 teaspoon vanilla
1 1/2 cups sifted enriched flour
1/2 teaspoon baking powder
1/4 teaspoon salt
3 tablespoons milk
3/4 teaspoon peppermint extract
Red food coloring

Directions:

Preheat oven to 375°F.

Cream shortening and sugar. Blend in egg yolk and vanilla. Sift dry ingredients; add alternately with milk. Add peppermint extract: mix well.

Add red food coloring to 1/2 of dough. Chill. Shape into candy canes with alternate red and white cookie dough and shape into 5 inch rolled strips. Twist into canes.

Bake at 375°F for about 10 minutes.

DIVINITY PUFFS
(Submitted by Valerie Peterson)

Ingredients:

2 cups white sugar
1/2 cup light corn syrup
1/2 cup water
Dash of salt
2 stiffly beaten egg whites
1 teaspoon vanilla extract

Directions:

Stir sugar into syrup, water and salt. Cook to dissolve sugar.
Then boil to 240°F. Slowly pour 1/3rd of syrup over stiffly
beaten egg whites, stirring constantly. Cook remaining syrup to
a hard-boiled stage 265°. Beat into egg white mixture. Continue
beating. When mixture holds shape, add vanilla. Drop from
teaspoon on waxed paper.

SNICKERDOODLES
(Submitted by Peggy Hyndman)

Ingredients:

1 cup butter (2 sticks)
1-1/2 cups sugar
2 large eggs
2 3/4 cups flour
2 teaspoons cream of tartar
1 teaspoon baking soda
1/4 teaspoon salt
3 tablespoons sugar
3 teaspoons cinnamon

Directions:

Mix butter, 1 1/2 cups sugar and eggs thoroughly in a large bowl.

Combine flour, cream of tartar, baking soda and salt in a separate bowl. Blend dry ingredients into butter mixture.

Chill dough, and chill an ungreased cookie sheet for about 10-15 minutes in the fridge.

Meanwhile, mix 3 tablespoons sugar, and 3 teaspoons cinnamon in a small bowl.
Scoop 1 inch balls of dough into the sugar/ cinnamon mixture.

Coat by gently rolling balls of dough in the sugar mixture.

Place on chilled ungreased cookie sheet, and bake 10 minutes at 375°F.

Remove from pan immediately.

SHARON'S CHOCOLATE CHIP COOKIES
(Submitted by Sharon Guagliardo)

Ingredients:

1 cup butter
3/4 cup sugar
1/2 cup brown sugar
2 eggs
2 teaspoons vanilla
2 1/4 cup flour
1/2 teaspoon baking soda
1 teaspoon salt
1 package chocolate chips
1/2 cup chopped walnuts

Directions:

Cream butter and sugars. Add eggs and vanilla. Mix the remaining dry ingredients together. Hand mix all ingredients together. Drop by rounded tablespoonful on ungreased cookies sheet and bake at 375ºF for 8 to 10 minutes. Makes about 3 dozen 2 inch cookies, or about 4 dozen 1 1/2 inch cookies.

ODESSA'S PUMPKIN COOKIES
(Submitted by Odessa Green)

Ingredients:

2 3/4 cups all-purpose flour
1 tsp baking soda
1 tsp baking powder
1 tsp cinnamon
1/2 tsp nutmeg
1/2 tsp ginger
1/2 tsp salt
1 stick butter
1 1/2 cups granulated cane sugar
1 1/2 cups pumpkin (not pumpkin pie mix)
1/2 tsp vanilla bean paste (or vanilla extract)
1 egg

Directions:

Preheat oven to 350ºF.

Combine flour, baking soda, baking powder, cinnamon, nutmeg, ginger and salt in a bowl mix until combined. Set aside.

In another bowl, cream sugar and butter until blended. Add the pumpkin, egg, and vanilla paste.
Add flour mixture slowly to pumpkin mixture. Drop by tablespoon onto cookie sheet. Bake 8-10 minutes or until light brown.

**Frost or serve plain

Sugar Cookie Cut-Outs
(Submitted by Pam Greenslate)

Ingredients:

1 1/2 cups powdered sugar
1 cup butter or margarine, softened
1 teaspoon vanilla
1/2 teaspoon almond extract
1 egg
2 1/2 cups Gold Medal™ all-purpose flour
1 teaspoon baking soda
1 teaspoon cream of tartar
Granulated sugar or colored sugar

Directions:

Mix powdered sugar, butter, vanilla, almond extract and egg in large bowl. Stir in remaining ingredients except granulated sugar. Cover and refrigerate at least 2 hours.

Heat oven to 375°F. Lightly grease cookie sheet.

Divide dough in half. Roll each half 1/4-inch-thick on lightly floured surface. Cut into desired shapes with 2- to 2 1/2-inch cookie cutters. Sprinkle with granulated sugar.

Place on cookie sheet. Bake 7 to 8 minutes or until edges are light brown. Remove from cookie sheet. Cool on wire rack.

DEBORAH GARNER

FLOURLESS PEANUT BUTTER CHOCOLATE CHIP COOKIES
(Submitted by Catherine Ojalvo)

Makes about 24 cookies

Ingredients:

1 cup super-chunky peanut butter
1 cup(packed) golden brown sugar
1 large egg
1 tsp. baking soda
1 tsp. vanilla extract
1cup miniature semisweet chocolate chips (about 6oz.)

Directions:

Preheat oven to 350ºF.

Mix first 5 ingredients in medium bowl. Mix in chocolate chips. Using moistened hands to form generous 1tablespoon dough for each cookie. Arrange on 2 ungreased baking sheets, spacing 2 inches apart.

Bake cookies until puffed, golden on the bottom and still soft in the center, about 12 minutes. Cool on sheets for 5 minutes. Transfer to racks and cool completely.

SNOWBALL COOKIES
(Submitted by Keri Knutson)

Ingredients:

2 cups all-purpose flour
1/2 cup ground almonds
1/4 teaspoon salt
1 cup butter, softened (2 sticks)
1/2 cup powdered sugar
3 teaspoons water
1 teaspoon almond extract
36 maraschino cherries, rinsed and patted dry
1 cup powdered sugar
1 tablespoon milk
2 cups coconut flakes

Directions:

Preheat oven to 350ºF.

Whisk together the flour, almonds, and salt.

In another mixing bowl, beat together butter and ½ cup sugar until light and creamy. Beat in the water and almond extract. Stir in the flour mixture until a dough forms.
Take tablespoons of dough and form a ball around each cherry. Place about 2 inches apart on baking sheets and bake for 18-20 minutes or until bottoms are browned. Remove to wire racks to cool completely.

To Glaze:
In a small bowl, mix a cup powdered sugar and 1 tablespoon milk. Dip the cooled cookies in the glaze and then roll in shredded coconut.

Makes 3 dozen cookies.

Deborah Garner

Grandma's Opera Fudge
(Submitted by Keri Knutson)

Ingredients:

2 cups sugar
1/2 cup milk
1/2 cup half-and-half
1 tablespoon light corn syrup
1/2 teaspoon salt
1 tablespoon butter
1 teaspoon vanilla
1/3 cup chopped candied red cherries

Directions:

Line a 5-3/4x3x2-inch loaf pan with foil or parchment paper and butter or spray with cooking spray.

In 2-quart saucepan, combine the sugar, milk, half-and-half, corn syrup and salt. Cook over medium heat, stirring constantly, until sugar dissolves and mixture comes to a boil. Keep boiling and stirring constantly until a candy thermometer reads 236°F (soft ball stage).

Remove saucepan from heat and add butter and vanilla. Cool at room temperature for 20 minutes, and then beat for five minutes. Stir in cherries. Pour into loaf pan and spread evenly. Place in refrigerator to cool. When chilled, remove fudge from pan and cut into pieces.

Makes 2 dozen pieces.

DUTCH SOUR CREAM COOKIES
(Submitted by Sherri Titus)

Ingredients:

1/2 cup soft butter (1 stick)
1 cup sugar
1 egg
1/2 teaspoon orange or lemon extract
1/2 teaspoon vanilla extract
3 cups all-purpose flour
1/4 teaspoon soda
1/4 cup sour cream

Directions:

Cream butter; gradually add sugar, beating until light and fluffy. Add egg and flavorings; beat well. Add flour, soda and sour cream.

Shape dough into a long roll, 2 inches in diameter; wrap in waxed paper, and chill 2 to 3 hours or until firm. Unwrap roll and cut into ¼ inch slices; place on ungreased cookie sheets.

Bake at 375°F for 8-10 minutes.

Yields 4 dozen

SOFT RAISIN COOKIES
(Submitted by Sherri Titus)

Ingredients:

3 1/4 cups flour
3 eggs
1 1/2 cup sugar
1 cup soft butter or margarine
2 teaspoons grated lemon peel
1 teaspoon baking soda
1 teaspoon vanilla extract
1/2 teaspoon salt
1 1/2 cup dark seedless raisins
1 1/2 cup chopped walnuts

Directions:

Make early in day or up to 2 weeks before serving.

Into large bowl – measure all but raisins and nuts. With mixer at low speed, beat ingredients until just mixed. Increase speed to medium and beat 2 minutes, occasionally scraping bowl with rubber spatula. Stir in raisins and nuts until they are well blended.

Preheat oven to 375°F. Drop batter by heaping tablespoon about 2 inches apart on greased cookie sheet.
Bake 12-15 minutes until lightly browned around the edges. With pancake turner, remove cookies to wire rack to cool completely. Store cookies in tightly covered container.

Makes 2 1/2 dozen.

BLUEBERRY OATMEAL COOKIES
(Submitted by Sherri Titus)

Ingredients

1 package wild blueberry muffin mix
3/4 cup quick-cooking oats
1/4 cup brown sugar
1/2 cup cooking oil
1 tablespoon milk
1 egg

Directions

In a medium bowl combine all but the blueberries: mix well.
Drop from a teaspoon onto an ungreased cookie sheet. Make
a deep depression in the center of each cookie and fill with 7-8
well-drained blueberries. Push dough from sides to cover berries
and pat down.

Bake at 375ºF for 8-10 minutes, until light brown.

ACKNOWLEDGEMENTS

When *Mistletoe at Moonglow*, the first Moonglow Christmas Novella, was released, future guests of the Timberton Hotel yearned to tell their stories, too. And so *Silver Bells at Moonglow* came to be. Heartfelt thanks go to D.A. Sarac at The Editing Pen for her excellent editing, as well as to Elizabeth Christy for initial developmental guidance. Carol Anderson's proofreading expertise provided final polishing touches. Sincere gratitude goes to Keri Knutson of Alchemy Book Covers for cover design, as well as to Leah Michelle Banicki and Tim Renfrow for formatting eBook and print editions. Jay Garner, Karen Putnam, and Carol Anderson all deserve credit for beta reading and plot suggestions.

Betty is always happy to share recipes from her annual cookie exchange. Yes, Betty is fictional, but the recipes are very real. So get out those holiday aprons and mixing bowls, and enjoy a few sweet treats. Thank you to the wonderful readers and authors who contributed: Kim McMahan Davis, Sue Doucette, Jan Harvey, Linda Smith, Kathy Turner, Frances Hampton, Odessa Green, Sharon Guagliardo, Peggy Hyndman, Pam Greenslate, Keri Knutson, Sherri Titus and Valerie Peterson.

RECIPE NOTES

RECIPE NOTES

RECIPE NOTES

RECIPE NOTES

Recipe Notes

Recipe Notes

Recipe Notes

CPSIA information can be obtained
at www.ICGtesting.com
Printed in the USA
LVHW101602211222
735605LV00003B/695

9 780996 996013